ONCE UPON A LUV

AN UNTOLD LOVE STORY

DR. VISHAL ANAND

Invincible Publishers

First Printing: 2019

ISBN: 978-93-89600-18-6

Invincible Publishers

Registered Address: 201A, SAS Tower, Sector 38, Gurgaon - 122003

For My Parents

&

My Family

ACKNOWLEDGEMENT

Acknowledgements are not easy to write. When there are people who believe in you more than you believe in yourself, words are not enough to give them their due. But words are all that I have at the moment. Needless to say, it wasn't possible for me to bring myself to write without not only the encouragement but insistence of my wife and my kids. They have been my inspiration, my backup, my advisors, my proofreaders and most importantly, my worst critics. Then there have been my friends and well-wishers to whom I would read the sample chapters and get their honest feedback. I would like to thank our close friends Ioana Apostal, Jayakumaran, Divyashree Kumari, Col. Deepak Bora and many others.

Special thanks to my wife Meena who has been rock solid through all my mood swings and lows. And to my daughter Kshitija who actually had the courage to tell a writer that his writings needed improvements on more occasion than one. Last but not the least; thanks are due to my son Shaurya who would always keep me on my toes through his continuous demands, bets and promises.

FOREWARD

We mostly see our soldiers in the light of their professional duties and forget that they too are humans with their own share of personal problems and struggles, just like us. Fighting enemies is not the only battle they are engaged in. Sometimes they win, sometimes they learn. This story is an effort to bring out the humane side of an army man.

Similarly, blaming the youth for their mistakes and indulgences has been the norm for long. Parents tend to forget that their children are also the reflection of their upbringing. This story is also the story of a young girl who could not get the support and guidance that she deserved during her teenage days.

When destiny brings both of them together, things happen. Some expected; others unexpected.

Sometimes we are just the slaves of our circumstances.

Table of Contents

CHAPTER 1

Calling Of The Mountains

Somewhere in the Himalayas...

It was a small sleepy hamlet high up in the mountains. Just before dawn, it became so cold that nobody would say it was summer. Because I was in the midst of it, I couldn't witness the glistening beauty of the mountains that would have been visible from a distance. But still, the lights from small habitation scattered over some distant slopes came through the glass panes of my window as I woke up to the sound of the alarm.

Being a mountaineer, I was in the habit of waking up at such odd hours. If your desire is to climb the virgin mountain peaks and return to your camping site before sunset, you need to do that. In the higher echelons of the mystic Himalayas where it gets prematurely dark, you have to start your day very early in fact.

Waking up before the sunrise has its perks as it gives you a chance to see the beauty of nature at its best. Sometimes, it is also a bait, but you are devoided from a chance of hindsight, and you won't remain alive after such misadventures.

I am a nature lover, and I intend to enjoy it for the longest possible time. Therefore, I sprang out of bed and forced myself to work. It was going to be a long tough day. Coming close to it, I looked out of my bedroom window. From the experience of the day, I knew it faced a deep valley, and some small village dwellings were scattered over the hills and beyond it. As I watched, a pattern of lights emerged out of the dark. It was like that of a women's necklace. If the mountain were considered as a queen, then this was a queen's necklace. In the darkness of my small room, I smiled at my thoughts and moved to the adjoining bathroom to wash off the remains of sleep.

As it was my habit before a climb, I removed the things from my rucksack on to the bed and started putting them back in an organized way one by one. Just for the security check, to be doubly sure because it can very well create a difference between your life and death. The ten essentials – map, compass, GPS, glacier glasses, Swiss knife, flashlight, extra batteries, matchsticks, fire starter, signalling mirror, first aid kit, duct tape, scissors, dry fruits, reflective blanket, an axe, a small shovel, and my personal favourite, a liquid stove. I was very particular about my stuff from a very young age. Now in my late twenties, it was somewhat difficult to change habits.

It was half-past five 'o clock in the morning when I left my room. Coming down the wooden floors of that small but cozy homestay accommodation, when I reached the shared reception area, the young fellow on the couch was apparently in the midst of his deep sleep for the night. It took a while for him to regain his consciousness. Just then, somewhere in the mountains, there was a little spark of lightning. I could see it through the glasses of the front door that opened on the outside. It was far away on the horizon.

"The weather looks ominous, Sir. You intend to leave?"

The boy asked while he was still rubbing his eyes.

"Sure as heaven."

I replied.

I was excited and nervous both at the same time. There was something about these mountains that always attracted my inner core. The rush of adrenaline before and the joy of achievement after a successful climb were my driving forces. But more than that, it always gave me a chance to meet myself on top of those mountains, to explore my own limits; I felt I was destined to climb them.

This mountain peak was not known when it came to climbing, and along with that, it was very dangerous. Some mountain peaks look deceptively small, but their geographical features make them utterly unconquerable. Everybody climbs Mount Everest, the Sagarmatha, while nobody has been able to conquer Mount Kailash, the Meru Parvat, the center of the Universe, and the abode of Shiva. High up in the Himalayas, you cannot miss his presence, my favourite God -Shiva. Sitting atop, alone, you can feel him around. One cannot survive without his blessings in the majestic Himalayas.

I looked towards the boy and from the wall behind him, found Lord Shiva smiling to me through a poster; I took it as a good omen. Handing over the room keys to him, I said,

"I have checked with the weather forecast, it's not going to rain before tonight, and they are quite accurate these days."

I smiled.

"Really, Sir, the weather changes very rapidly in these mountains."

He looked unconvinced as he said that. A bolt of faint lightning cracked again in the horizon.

"I am not going that way."

I looked in the direction of the lightning.

"Please keep my tea ready in the afternoon, would you?"

While saying that, I stepped out of my accommodation and was at once welcomed by the sudden gust of cold wind. The dimly lit lanes of that small village were devoid of any living soul at that hour. Even the mountain dogs, quite active during the day, were lying hidden somewhere. Once again, I was about to begin my climb under the stars that were shining brightly overhead.

It happened when I was half done. For once, the weather seemed to have beaten the humans at the game of changing colours in no time. The wind changed its course, bringing the faraway clouds to just where I was. To begin with, I couldn't fathom their gravity; I became aware of how they were getting denser with each passing moment at the daybreak. I looked at my watch, it was nine in the morning, and the daylight was almost nonexistent.

I did a rare miscalculation then. The summit was still a few hours of the climb away according to my normal speed. I thought I would still be able to make it and return safely before the weather could pose a threat. Hardly half an hour more was left for me to complete the climb when the rain happened, and it turned to snow in no time. In the beginning, the snowflakes were soft and tiny. If I had not been aware of the impending danger, I would have enjoyed them. Suddenly the weather got warmer, and I instinctively knew it was time to make a retreat. The hamlet below, from where I came wasn't visible anymore.

As I embarked on the descent, the snow started falling heavily. I tried to increase my pace, but the fresh snow beneath my feet didn't allow me to do so. I looked for the trail that I had taken on ascend, the only thing I could see was the white sheet of snow. I suddenly slipped and fell several feet below. I tried to get up but felt an excruciating pain in my right ankle. With my movements hampered, I struggled to move down. Within a short span of half an hour, the situation turned from a desperate moment into a hopeless one. The winds pressed hard against my face as I tried to look in all directions.

In those moments of despair, I tried to remember Shiva, the Lord of Himalayas. Please help me! I pleaded. Suddenly, from the corner of my eyes, I sensed some movement. I instinctively moved my sight in that direction, but I couldn't see anything clearly. I moved some paces, there was unmistakably something there. A shiver ran down my spine, and it wasn't due to cold. What if it turns out to be a snow leopard? I stopped, trying to figure out the danger. I have heard the stories of leopards roaming in those areas. There were some pine trees over the slopes, their conical leaves allowing most of the snow to fall through them and all around me. For a change, I tried to get some benefit out of them. It was good that my mind was still working, and did not slow down by the freezing cold and chilly circumstances. I hid behind one of the nearby trees. Although I wasn't in a position to do much against a wild animal, at least my survival instincts were in place.

I missed them on the first go, they were so hazy. But I got the idea that I could move closer and that I did. Suddenly they were just in front of me, the most beautiful pair of golden deer you would ever see. They shone brightly, despite there being no Sun. They were agile, with bright, beautiful eyes looking directly towards me, as if they wanted to say something. It was such a mesmerising moment that I lost the thought of impending danger. Hooked to them, I moved closer. They ran away, just to stop again after covering only few paces. It happened many times until I got the idea that they wanted me to follow them. Struggling all the time, I tried my best to keep pace with that pair of mysterious creatures.

Amidst heavy snow, that small journey took me somewhere; I did not know how it was going to change my life then. The most important journey of my life, although astonishingly small, made under grave circumstances, assisted by a mysterious pair of golden deer only to be found in higher Himalayas took me to a cave that was hidden somewhere in those mountains.

It was a small cave; there was nothing spectacular about it. What was spectacular was the fact that once being inside the cave, the beautiful pair of deer vanished. I stepped into the cave, and there was nothing inside it. I took out the flashlight from the side pocket of my bag and used it to look around; they were nowhere to be seen. But being inside that cave brought me instant relief from cold and snow, it was rather cosy inside. I put my bag down in the middle of that natural structure. It wasn't more than 25 feet deep and half that wide. I was dead tired and cold by now, so I removed my backpack and sat down with my back to the wall of the cave. I took out the liquid fuel lamp, and I kept it on the white gas to get some warmth.

I remained like that for a while. It was so silent inside; it was only obvious to become unaware of the outside turmoil. No doubt the sages in ancient times loved to meditate in such places. But I was still shivering from cold. When it got bearable after a while, I began to look around. I suddenly noticed that there was a pile of what looked like garbage at the far end of the cave. Holding the flashlight, I went close to it. Many things were scattered all around, it looked like some personal belongings. It contained some pieces of logwood; there was a rugged mat and a few broken earthen utensils. There lied a small cloth bag as well, similar to the ones fashionably carried by the journalists and writers of the seventies and the eighties. It was clear that the cave was inhabited by someone in the past. But looking at its present condition, it would have been decades since someone had put his foot inside it again. Out of curiosity, I moved through the scattered garbage.

Suddenly, as I lifted it, the cloth bag felt heavy, there

was something inside it. As I turned it upside down, an old dilapidated diary fell close to my feet. I was surprised as I picked up the diary. It looked old and was in bad shape. I put that diary on the floor and sat down beside it. Holding the flashlight in one hand, as I flipped through its pages, it became clear that the contents of the diary, though torn from places, were mostly safe. It looked like someone's personal diary.

It was still snowing heavily outside. I brought the fuel stove close by and pushing my back to the wall of that cave, began to go through the contents of that diary, completely oblivious of the fact that I have found a personal treasure.

I did not know for how long I read like that; it must have been more than a few hours. I was so engrossed in its contents that I stopped only because I felt as if someone was watching me through the opening of the cave. I immediately looked up, there was no one to be seen, what I saw instead was clear weather outside. The snow had stopped, nobody could say how grave the weather was a few hours ago. I got up, it was time to leave. I put the diary carefully inside my backpack and prepared to leave. From the opening of the cave, I turned to have one final look inside the place that had saved my life that day.

As I made my descent, I had a feeling that someone was following me. I abruptly stopped in my tracks to look back and found the same beautiful pair of Kasturi deer looking towards me. It seemed they were following me. Their eyes were hooked to mine, from what were hardly twenty paces of distance. They were standing at the entrance of the cave. As I waved towards them, they turned and went away. Miracles were still coming my way.

I was having much more difficulty on the descent than I had anticipated. No trails existed anymore, it was snow all around. As I was getting frustrated with my efforts, I heard someone call my name. I shouted back and kept going until I saw a group of uniformed men ascending in my direction.

Seeing me struggling to move through the heavy snow, the men in front, probably their leader, shouted,

"Please stay there; we are coming to get you."

I stopped my efforts. As they came closer, I could recognise that they were a team from NDRF, the disaster relief force. My prayers were answered. I looked towards heaven to thank Lord Shiva.

"Sir, are you alright?"

The man asked.

"Yeah, I am, even better now."

I tried to smile as I said that.

"We were informed by the people you are staying with. It was a massive storm."

The man said.

"Thanks for saving me," I said and followed the brave soldiers.

Getting back to my room was such a relief. It was one such moment when I wasn't successful, but I was not disappointed. I suspected that everything was driven by some unknown force and it was destined to happen the way it did.

It was almost dark outside when I got out of my dreamy sleep. I have seen the same pair of golden deer in my dreams; they were looking towards me as if they wanted to convey something. I should have slept for several hours, I was dead tired. I asked for some tea and homely cooked food and took out the diary I have found in that mysterious cave. Intrigued by its contents, I intended to finish reading it as soon as possible.

It was going to be a long night.

I did not know at what time I went to sleep again. The good thing was, most of my questions were answered that night. The diary contained comprehensive details. But there were still some queries in my mind, some missing links. I was feeling a great urge from within to find answers.

Still early in the morning, I came down to the reception, it was time to leave. The same young man was sitting behind the desk in the lobby. Probably he was the one who intimated the NDRF about me.

“I cannot thank you enough for saving my life,”

I said as I approached him.

“It’s my duty, Sir. I got worried about you as the snowstorm worsened. It really looked bad from here.”

He replied, pointing in the direction of the summit.

“That it surely was,”

I answered smiling towards him.

“Are you leaving Sir?”

He inquired.

I nodded.

“For how long have you been in this town?”

I asked him suddenly.

He stopped preparing the bills and looking up to me, replied,

"I was born here, Sir. As far as I know, we are living here for ages."

"Do you know something about the cave up there?"

When I asked him that question, it was entirely based on some intuition. Even I was surprised why I said that. And I was more than astonished with his reply. He said,

"Maybe you're talking about the Con man's Cave, Sir."

"Con man's Cave?"

I was puzzled.

"Yes, Sir, Con man's Cave. We all have heard about it, but nobody goes there anymore."

"Means?"

It was getting interesting, I asked impatiently.

"Maybe it's a bad omen to talk about it, Sir. I don't know."

The interest of the boy in the subject was nowhere close to mine. He went back to preparing my bill.

But he had got me hooked.

"Then who would know?"

I blurted out suddenly.

"Maybe my grandfather. He was the village headmen when that cave came in the reckoning."

"Where can I find him?"

I was getting increasingly impatient. I could feel the hair on my forearms rising in anticipation.

"He remains mostly at home these days. You see, he is an old man now, Sir."

"Can I meet him?"

I enquired.

"If you want, I can take you there. My home is nearby. But you will have to give me a few minutes to finish the work. I will be off duty in a short while."

'I can wait for a lifetime, man.' I said silently to myself and sat down to wait.

The boy's home was at the far end of the village. We crossed many lanes and by-lanes, going up and down time and again. These hilly villages possess a soul of their own. Surrounded by fresh snow-clad mountains from all sides, I felt a certain kind of tranquillity engulfing my being. The Himalayas were looking majestic, and I soaked in their grandeur. The peak that I went out to conquer the day before was shining like a precious jewel on top of a crown in the sunshine.

The boy's home was a typical mountain dwelling. On the outskirts of the village, it was a double storied house with carved wooden windows upfront that were painted brightly. There was a cow tied in the open front space on the left corner of the building. Cattle feed was stored next to it. On the right side and opposite to it, there were what appeared to be toilets outside the house. Just in front of the house in the middle, an old man was sitting on a charpoy, puffing on a 'Bidi'. Some women were working in small fields at a distance. The boy went ahead and touching the feet of the old man, he said,

"Bubu, this Saheb is staying at the house. He wants to know something about our village, so I have brought him here."

The old man with great wrinkles looked up to me and asked,

"What is it that you want to know Saheb?"

It might have been a rare occasion when someone had come asking about the village, for the old man and looked utterly confused.

Measuring my words, I answered,

"Baba, I want to know about the Con man's cave up there."

I gestured towards the peak.

The old man looked up. He did not say anything for a very long time. He was testing my patience. Finally he said,

"*Saheb,* it has been for the first time in so many years that someone has come asking for that cave. It has been a very long time, more than twenty years since we saw the last of it. You won't gain anything out of it, only bad things would happen."

The old man seemed reluctant to come up with the information.

It was getting unbearable. To loosen him up, I tried to push him further,

"Baba, I want to know why it is called the Con man's Cave."

I waited and waited for an answer. Perhaps he was scared to say anything. I remembered the boy who had told me it was a bad omen to talk about the cave. He seemed to be measuring the pros and cons for a while.

The inhabitants of Himalayan regions have always been a great host. They can go to great lengths to make their guests happy. I knew it due to my years of experience of travelling and climbing in the Himalayas.

To this date, I cannot say with certainty why he decided to tell me the story. All I can say is, perhaps the divine force was working all the time, clearing every hurdle that came my way.

It took more than half an hour for the old village headman to finish his story of the 'Con man's Cave' in his own style. It answered many of my questions and confirmed many of my newly acquired facts. He ended the story by saying,

"After that Saheb, nobody went into that cave again. The whole of the village was fooled greatly."

I stood up to leave; there was nothing left to be known. Now I knew two stories, one that was told by an old man and the other, written in an unknown, depleted diary. I thanked the old man, and as I was about to climb up the road, I felt an urge from within. I suddenly said,

"Have you ever thought that perhaps nobody fooled you, not even someone whom you call the Con man?"

To say that the old village headman was greatly puzzled would have been an understatement. He just kept looking at my face. I felt an obligation to say something.

"I will come again, Baba."

I climbed up the road. A new journey was waiting for me to begin.

The taxi that I had booked in advance took me to Rishikesh, the holy city situated on the banks of the sacred Ganges. I visited many places, travelled extensively

in northern hilly states of the country for the next two months. The diary was my constant companion, my prized possession and I read and reread it several times. I met many new people, I didn't know existed. I went to the capital city, my quest took me to some government establishments as well, where I was forced to shell out money to get the information I required. I even went outside the country, it was imperative.

These few months have been the most intriguing months of my life. Today, sitting in my study I can hear the droplets of water hitting the window panes. It has been raining heavily outside. The weather forecast says it's going to remain like this for the next couple of days. I intend to use this time to tell you the story. I am again going to believe the weatherman. I have been fooled by many people in my life. But I have always ensured that my bad experiences shouldn't come in my way of maintaining a belief.

And today, I do believe there is a story out there that deserves to be told.

Before sunrise, when I embarked on my ascent to conquer the summit, little did I know that the next few hours were going to change my life. Inside an unknown dark mountain cave up in the Himalayas, a story was waiting for me. It was waiting to see the light of the day and also the truth...

CHAPTER 2

When Someone Fell For Words

Military College of Telecommunication Engineering (MCTE)

Mhow, Madhya Pradesh. 1990.

Mhow is a small Cantonment town that was founded by a British named John Malcolm way back in 1818 when the British defeated the Holkar Marathas, and the Treaty of Mandsaur came into effect. It was also the headquarters of the 5th Division of Southern Command during the British regime. Today, it is home to three premier training institutes of the Indian Army. Besides MCTE, it also houses The Infantry School and The Army War College.

Major Veer Pratap Singh was an instructor of the Faculty of Combat Communication Engineering at MCTE, the alma mater of Corps of Signals in the Indian Army.

It was a beautiful February evening. The spring was just about to set in. The evening breeze still possessed a cool tinge to it. The Petunia flowers were still in blossom on both sides of the passage that led to the building. It was a typical army styled building with slanting asbestos roofs and a veranda upfront. A sentry was standing at the entrance of the office that announced the name of its occupant 'Major V.P. Singh, S.M.' the S.M. referred to the 'Sena Medal' that he had won the previous year in Kashmir. The present posting was a 'soft duty' after two years of nullifying the nefarious plans of Pakistani militants in a dangerous valley that once was known as 'paradise on earth.'

Way past the working hours, the Major was still at his desk as usual when someone called up from the entrance door,

"Good evening Major. May I disturb you for a while?"

The Major looked up from the piles of papers in front of him and seeing his colleague and his batchmate who was also his best friend peeping from the door, smiled and said,

"Oh. Rajesh! Come on in."

Major V.P. Singh was a very handsome man. Having started his career early and graduating through National Defence Academy at Khadakwasla near Pune, he was just in his late twenties. Almost six feet tall with athletic built, he was an avid sportsman. His sharp, prominent eyes were the highlights of his intelligent looking face. He carried an air of authority and a no-nonsense attitude around his demeanour.

Taking a chair and sitting across the desk, Major Rajesh said to his friend,

"So the decorated Major is still deep in work so late in the evening?"

"Not really. The Sahayak has brought the regular fan mail; I was just going through the same."

There was a file marked as 'Fan' that he was holding in his hand. He kept a letter inside it.

"Yet another letter from the same fan, Veer?"

Major Rajesh asked as he saw the letter.

"Yeah, it is the same."

"You always keep all the letters safe from this particular fan."

"She is different Rajesh. Being so intelligent and sensitive at such a young age is extremely rare. Look what she has written this time…"

Major Veer took out the letter he had just put in the file and began to read,

"Dear Major, from where does a battle-hardened army man acquires the emotions that you bring to your writings. Please throw some light on the same some day."

"She has also written one of her own couplets."

The Major looked up to his friend. He gestured to go ahead.

"She writes, 'Its love that flows through the veins,

You call it blood, by what means?' "

"Shiraon Mein jo behta hai, wo ishq ka dariya hai!

"Wo isko lahu kehte hain, ye unka nazariya hai!"

"Talented, she is!"

Major Rajesh said.

"Extremely talented."

Major Veer replied.

Major Rajesh got up from his chair. Coming to the other side of the table and close to where his friend was sitting, he said,

"Veer, you are a famous poet and a writer, and you get regularly published in papers and magazines. You have got numerous fans. I have seen you collecting all the letters from this girl and putting them safe. But you have never written a reply mail."

"I never write a reply because I do not possess an answer, Rajesh. She is my biggest fan. Sometimes, fans also share their struggles and difficulties with me. I cannot afford to get involved in them. I can feel pity, I get inspired and I can certainly write about them, but that's the end to it. This girl has got a dysfunctional family. We all have to fight our own battles, Rajesh."

Major Rajesh was extremely fond of his best friend. They have met for the first time at the National Defence Academy when both of them were rookie cadets trying to survive the rigour of punishing military training. Veer was always good at almost everything; he had helped him in numerous ways throughout the years, no less when they both joined as officers. Veer was extremely helpful and considerate for his colleagues and subordinates alike and he was respectful towards his seniors. It was his thorough professionalism that would set him apart as a soldier. Rajesh could not fathom why God chose to deny him peace at the personal front while blessing him with everything professionally.

Major Veer's face bore a grim look. He had lost his family a long way back. Brought up by some distant relatives from his mother's side that were kind enough to raise him as their own son, Veer now possessed a firsthand experience of owning a dysfunctional family, he himself was heading one at the moment.

CHAPTER 3

Dance Of The Circumstances

Mussoorie, Uttarakhand. North India.

1990.

Mussoorie is called the 'Queen of Hills'. It can be like any other hill station but for its awesome weather especially during the summer months, it is like coming to a different world for the tourists and vacationers from all over the country. Clouds keep on coming all through the day, sometimes even getting inside the houses. It's a small town with less than fifty thousand population, where everyone knows everyone else. Most of the Mall Road is full of hotels, restaurants and shops catering to the waves of tourists for the most part of the year. It remains lively throughout the day and half of the night.

But for its inhabitants, real Mussoorie lies in lanes and by-lanes just above and below the Mall Road. Away from the chaos, people live in small wooden houses and shop at the local market where only a few tourists would visit.

It was one such small house, with a slanting tin roof. Despite its ordinary structure, the house looked beautiful because of pretty flowers growing all around it. All sorts of waste bottles and pots were used to grow the plants in their cavities–empty cold drink bottles, talcum powder cans, used containers of chocolates and cookies and paint boxes, all were tastefully decorated with beautiful flowering plants, giving it a distinct look and identity among neighbouring houses.

It was the morning time and Bhumi was getting late for school. Her final exams of the intermediate class were just around the corner and she did not want to miss her classes. As she hurriedly packed her school bag, her mother shouted from inside the bathroom,

"Bhumi, O Bhumi! Where the hell are you?"

"I am getting ready for school Ma."

Putting her books in the school bag, Bhumi replied in haste. She was a beautiful young mountain girl, all seventeen years of age. Her cheeks were pink and her features were sharp. Her eyes were moist and innocent like that of a small kid and her simplicity was one of her numerous attractions.

"Prepare four 'chapatis' for your brother and sister and four for me, would you?"

Her mother was shouting.

"How can I? It's already late."

She pleaded.

"To hell with your school. Do as I say, otherwise you know what I can do."

Her mother shouted menacingly.

"I am already late for school."

There was frustration in her voice.

"Don't you tell me this rubbish; I am fed up of working nonstop for this family. Do as I have told you, then you can go wherever you want to, even to hell."

Her mother was furious.

Utterly disappointed that she was, Bhumi put down her school bag and went to the makeshift kitchen that occupied one side of the veranda. As she began to knead the flour, her best friend Sunita started calling her name. She was standing on the street that was on a higher plane, just in front of Bhumi's house.

"Bhumi, Bhumi. Hurry up, would you? Otherwise, we will miss school again today?"

She was saying.

"You go Suni, I will just follow you. I have to prepare breakfast first, otherwise..."

Bhumi was cut short by the shout from inside the bathroom,

"Whom are you talking to? Now you have the time for all this and you have all the excuses for anything I tell you to do, haan!"

Sunita threw up her hands in the air in exasperation.

"Hurry up Bhumi, I will move slowly."

She said as she stood up to leave. Bhumi increased her pace as she fought to control her tears. These days, she was finding it increasingly difficult to deal with the escalating demands of her stepmother. She was a stereotype stepmother as they are depicted on the silver screens and soap operas.

The school gate was already closed by the time Bhumi approached it hurriedly. She couldn't do anything about it, she was utterly disappointed. She stood there for a while and then started dragging her feet in the direction from where she came.

On her way back, Bhumi didn't feel like going back to home at once. The way back passed through beautiful Deodar trees that stood on either side of the road. There was a place just beside the road and an old Deodar tree stood there majestically. That was her favourite spot. Many times, coming back from the school, she and Sunita would sit there for a while and talk about everything. She was feeling extremely low and although Sunita wasn't there to give her company, she still sat down under her favourite tree for a while. She began scribbling in her diary; it was her habit from a very early age.

She wrote…

"I missed the school once again. However hard I may try, I would never win let alone the heart, even the sympathy of my mother. She never understands that I need to work hard in my studies…"

She kept on writing for the next half hour, it was her only solace. There were very few people with whom she could share her plights and sufferings and as they came thick and fast, Bhumi had turned to writing. She felt that she could pour everything out without being judged or condemned. She was a sensitive and emotional girl who could easily be misunderstood. It was not long before her diary became a part of her and her constant companion.

Suddenly Bhumi sensed that there were some young boys roaming around looking at her suspiciously. She hurriedly packed her diary into her bag and left for home. She ignored the comments of the boys.

Her mother was furious as usual when Bhumi reached home.

"Where have you been loafing around, haan?"

She shouted as soon as she saw her.

"I was late for school, again."

Bhumi replied plainly.

"Being late and deliberately getting late are two different things. Even if the school was closed, is this the time to come back home?"

The mother was nagging continuously.

"I didn't feel like coming back straightaway."

Bhumi could feel the anger building up inside her.

"Precisely. Because you want readymade food. I am a servant to this house, na?"

Her mother shouted back. As she was about to go more, a middle aged man entered the house, coming down from the street.

"Why there is so much noise inside?"

He enquired.

Before Bhumi could say anything, her mother began to say,

"Now only you can make her understand. She has again missed the school. When I ask her to be attentive and regular, she doesn't like it at all. I am always the vamp."

She was polite and was trying to pose as her well-wisher. Bhumi was startled to see the change in her behaviour. She couldn't say anything. It was also not her nature to aggravate matters. Even her mother knew that.

Once mother went inside, Bhumi's father went to her, making her sit beside him on the doorsteps.

"Apparently the princess is very angry."

He said politely as he caressed her hairs with his fingers.

"But she is your mother. She won't think anything bad about you."

He was trying to pacify her.

Bhumi looked into his eyes, and sadly murmured,

"She is not my mother Papa. My mother is up there with God, she is just your wife."

Bhumi was only seven years old when her mother passed away after a prolonged illness. Her father struggled to raise his only daughter but when dealing with her along with his government job as a primary school teacher became too much of a challenge and more importantly, when the constant pressure from relatives to remarry couldn't be brushed aside anymore, he got a new mother to Bhumi and a new wife to himself. To begin with, he had explained everything to her before marriage, and she looked a very understanding lady. She had promised to look after Bhumi as her own daughter. But everything changed as soon as she got pregnant for the first time. And it worsened after she gave birth to a boy. Bhumi, who once was the cynosure of all eyes, would feel immense pain as almost everyone coming to their home began to ignore her. They all would only love her small brother. Even the sweets they bought were meant for the little one, it seemed.

Bhumi tried to love her sibling, she was fond of small kids, but her mother created all the differences. The only saving grace was her father, but then his wife would only behave entirely different in front of him; she would be so sweet towards her. Sometimes, she suspected that father knew everything but was helpless. Bhumi would generally keep quite. Even her stepmother sensed that and made good use of the fact to her advantage.

Bhumi had begun to feel guilty of blurting out against her.

Her father couldn't say anything; he began to look in another direction. But he regained his composure quickly and said,

"Do you know why I am early today?"

"Why? Your school might have got over before time."

"By no means. I took a half-day leave. Actually I had to go to the market to get something."

"What?"

"This is it."

Father took out a magazine from his shoulder bag. It was the latest edition of a monthly Hindi magazine "Gruhshoba."

As soon as Bhumi saw the magazine in her Father's hands, her face started beaming with delight. She almost snatched the magazine from her father, saying,

"When did it arrive? Papa, you are too good. I love you. Thank you…Thank you…"

She ran inside the house, excitedly.

It brought a brief smile on her father's face. He wished to put the whole world into her lap, this was the least he could do.

Bhumi threw her school bag away as soon as she reached her room and lay down on the couch with the magazine in her hands. She started turning the pages vigorously, searching for her favourite article. There it was, and she smiled for the first time that day. It contained a new poem written by Veer Pratap Singh. She read it intently, she read it aloud and then she started reading it melodiously. Holding the magazine close to her chest, she lied down on her back and looking towards the ceiling, suddenly murmured,

"How beautiful do you write, dear army man? How do you look, by the way?"

Then behaving just like a teenager, she frowned and throwing the magazine aside, snarled at herself,

"How would I know? I do not know. You won't tell me anything. I know nothing, huh!"

CHAPTER 4

The Destined Encounter

Mhow, Madhya Pradesh.

It was a party at the Army Officers Club. The catering was outdoors. As per the army tradition, the ladies were gathered on one side of the brightly decorated lawns away from their officer husbands, who were standing as groups in circles all over the place. Brightly coloured flower pots were put all around the lawns. An orchestra was playing at one corner, it was organised at an elevated stage. The 'Sahayaks' were roaming around carrying the food items in the treys covered with velvety linen. There was an open bar set up at one end of the lawn, catering to the thirst of men and women alike.

Major Veer and Major Rajesh were standing with fellow officers close to where the bar was.

Major Rajesh was speaking joyously,

"Poet Sir, even I have written a couplet today."

"Couplets are said, not written."

Someone interrupted.

"O.k., o.k., I have said a couplet then."

Maj. Rajesh said hurriedly.

"Irshaad."

Another officer said, smiling.

"Arz Kia hai,"

"*Khujli...* "

As Maj. Rajesh began his poem, someone interrupted,

"*Khujli?*"

"Yes Sir, *khujli*"

"Wah-wah "

Someone proclaimed.

" khujli jitna khujao, Badti jaati hai.

Aur

"Biwi jitna manao, bigadti Jaati hai!"

Maj. Rajesh ended.

"Very good. Very good."

Everyone clapped. Maj. Veer was smiling.

Inadvertently, his eyes went towards his wife and found her talking to a young captain very intimately. She was having wine and looked drunk. She wore the quite modern dress even by army standards and seemed less than decent with her gestures.

He wasn't impressed. Sensing the disapproval of his friend towards the ways of his wife, Maj. Rajesh took him by his elbow to a side and away from the group and murmured,

"Veer. Why don't you make her see sense? You must talk to her about this kind of behaviour. This is not good."

"I have done everything that I could Rajesh. She is hell-bent on destroying me."

"But this is ridiculous. There must be some reason to it."

Rajesh was saying.

"There is a reason Rajesh. You see, I do not remember my real parents. I was too young when I lost them in an accident. I was then adopted by my wife's parents. They brought me up well, I will always be indebted to them for everything they did to me. They desired to get their only daughter married to me. They thought it would make her see sense. I couldn't say no, they did so much for me as my Godparents. Now she thinks I have destroyed her life. It's revenge, Rajesh."

"But...

As Maj. Rajesh was about to say something, someone called Veer,

"Where are you, Maj. Veer? Everybody is waiting for your latest poem. Come on. Get the party on fire."

Many more people started requesting. With his wife looking distastefully towards him, Maj. Veer took to the stage.

It was breakfast time at Veer's residence. All dressed up, he was silently eating the food. His wife was talking loudly on the phone that was kept at one corner of the room. She was fixing some plans for a party with her friend. She was loud, and she was boisterous. Maj. Veer was apparently disturbed.

As soon as she put the phone down, Maj. Veer, unable to contain his anger, blurted out suddenly,

"Why don't you ever get tired of all this partying?"

She had started to walk away; suddenly she turned back and curtly said,

"In fact, I am sick and tired of you Maj. Veer."

"Then why don't you spare me?"

"I will spare you, once I get my dues, mister. Now it's upto you to decide whether you are going to pay me or you intend to leave it to the courts to decide. I won't even let you have a divorce before that, you understand?"

"But I don't have the kind of money you demand."

Veer said frustratingly.

"That's your headache. My parents gave all the money to you, didn't they? With the condition that I should be trapped with you all through my life, otherwise, I would get nothing. I will teach you a lesson for this treachery, you'll see!"

She shouted and went away swiftly, banging the door behind her. What she had said was true; her parents had set such conditions. But it wasn't Veer's fault; he was just repaying the debts of her parents. They were great human beings, and it was difficult for Veer to think about reasons for their only daughter to be so unlike her parents. He was left sitting motionless and all by himself, having no solution to his woes.

Bhumi was trying to study in her room when her stepmother yelled at her.

"Bhumi, bring me a glass of water."

She got up and handed the glass of water to her mother, who was sitting with a group of neighbouring ladies in the veranda.

As soon as she tried to get back to her studies, she was called again,

"Bhumi, don't you have the etiquettes to prepare some tea for your aunties?"

Her stepmother shouted, brushing away the slight protests from one of the ladies.

"I was preparing for my exams."

Despite being much disturbed, she tried to be polite.

"You see, as soon as I tell this girl even some little work, she will start studying. I am fed up of her."

She could hear her mother telling her friends. They murmured in acceptance of the truth.

Her eyes filled with tears, Bhumi started to prepare some tea. As soon as tea was served, she took her books and began to leave the house.

"Now where are you going?"

Her mother shouted from behind.

"I am going to Sunita's place to check for today's classwork."

She said plainly and went away, leaving behind her stepmother cursing under her breath.

Sunita's house was just across the street. As she entered her friend's house, she saw her mother working in the kitchen.

"Where Is Sunita Aunty?"

She inquired.

"She is studying up there on the roof, beta."

Bhumi silently wished she should have got a mother like her. People born around the turn of the 21st century might find it hard to believe, but there was a time not so long ago when one could go to her friend's house unannounced and completely devoid of uncomfortable formalities of present times. Those were the times when a friend's house was just like one's own. It was more real for the communities of small towns. For Bhumi, Sunita's house was just like that, it was a house of respite.

Sunita was sitting on the floor, as soon as she saw her best friend coming, a broad smile broke upon her lips, but sensing her to be in a foul mood, she tried to be funny,

"Who has thrown my topper's mood for a six, Haan?"

"It's happening all the time these days. That lady wouldn't allow me to study at all."

Bhumi said disappointingly.

"Let her be like that only. You know she won't mend her ways. Never mind, we will study here."

Sunita tried to pacify her. Bhumi could not dare think of her life without Sunita. She was the bright spot in her rather grey life. They were not only the neighbours and classmates, but they were also soulmates. She could only ignore all the tantrums and punishments meted out by her stepmother because Sunita was always there with her bright smile and positive attitude. Away from public glare and scrutiny of family members, they both used to have their share of fun and freedom together.

"But, first of all, tell me the latest about the Fauzi uncle."

She was saying.

The mention of Maj. Veer brought a smile on Bhumi's lips. As she was about to say something, she suddenly realised the humour in Sunita's words. She stopped smiling and feigning anger, shouted,

"What did you just call him by the way?"

"I called uncle, uncle only."

Sunita teased her further.

"He can only be uncle to you, bastard."

Bhumi tried to beat her up with the book in her hand. But it was only a game played between two best friends and the only respite in what were rather dull days in Bhumi's life.

It was evening time. As soon as her father was home from his duty, Bhumi came running excitedly towards him. She was watering the flowers that were so dear to her.

"Papa, papa..."

She even threw away the water pipe.

"Easy beta. Let me come in first..."

Her father laughed as he came down from the street and into the house.

"Papa, I have been invited to recite my poems at the Town Hall this coming Sunday. They are organising an all India Kavi Sammelan on that day."

She was babbling.

"Really? Now that's some news."

A broad smile danced on her Father's lips.

Suddenly, her mother called her from inside,

"Bhumi, this Sunday, your Uncle is coming home with family. I need your help in preparing food for them, don't you forgot it this time."

Apparently, she had overheard the talk between the father and the daughter.

Bhumi's face dropped down with disappointment. She turned to her father saying,

"Now see Papa, she always does that to me. Papa, it's a part of the Mussoorie Festival, and It is a new initiative by the government, to promote tourism here. So many big poets are coming to participate; I won't get a chance like this again Papa."

She pleaded.

"You don't worry beta. Prepare well. Your mother will not pose a problem."

Getting the assurance from her father, Bhumi started beaming again. She was one such girl who would be happy by small acts of love and care. As her father tried to get inside the house, she called,

"Papa?"

Her father stopped.

"Would you come and see me perform?"

She asked.

"Beta who would stop me?"

He smiled and went inside the house. Her eyes were filled with tears of joy.

Town Hall, Mussoorie.

A banner hanging outside the building read,

"Mussoorie Festival welcomes you all To the first All India Kavi Sammelan and Mushaira"

The main hall of the building was filled with local audiences and tourists alike. All the participating poets were sitting in a semicircle on the stage. The special guests and dignitaries were seated on the first row just close to the stage. Bhumi's father and Sunita were sitting in between the crowd of people towards the back rows of the auditorium, their faces beaming with excitement. Some local press photographers were clicking the pictures, hanging around the stage close to where the compère was announcing,

"Ladies and gentlemen, I am happy to announce that our chief guest for today's inauguration is arriving in a short while from now. In the meantime, I would like to present before you, one of the brightest upcoming young poetess from our city, our very own Miss Bhumi Singh."

Everyone clapped, but none more than Sunita and her father. Hearing her name being announced, Bhumi stepped onto the stage, folded her hands and bowed to the audiences. Seeing Sunita waving vigorously and whistling at the same time, her lips broke into a smile. She looked so beautiful that the whole stage came alive with her bright smile and twinkling eyes.

The compère was giving an introduction…

"Miss Bhumi is a first-year student of literature at Mussoorie College. You will be delighted to know that she is also our topper of Intermediate boards. Apart from a brilliant scholar, she is also an upcoming writer. So here she is with her poems..."

Everyone clapped.

The mike was handed over to her.

As she was about to begin with her recital, there was a commotion at the entrance to the hall. It seemed some important dignitaries were making an entry. She had to stop as the compère came rushing, asked for the mike and made an announcement-

"Ladies and gentlemen, our chief guest for today, Lt. Col. Veer Pratap Singh has arrived amongst us. Currently posted at Chakrata, Lt. Col. Singh, as we all know, is a famous writer and a poet. He has been published extensively over the years and has several books to his credit."

The chief guest was facilitated by the organisers and guided to his place in the meantime. As for Bhumi, she couldn't believe what she had just heard. The organisers had kept the name of their chief guest a secret; she was utterly unaware that her favourite poet, the one she had been admiring secretly since her early teenage years would suddenly be revealed and that too under such circumstances. She couldn't believe he would be there among the audience with her being on to the big stage for the very first time.

She could feel her legs trembling and palms perspiring despite the weather being cold inside the hall. She had never seen him, not even in pictures. She knew him only by his words, and they were beautiful. If it was possible for someone to fall for words, then her tender heart had fallen for his writings years ago. She looked towards Sunita; at least she wasn't looking nervous. Instead, she seemed utterly excited. She was gesturing her to be strong, it brought some self-belief back into her.

Garnering all the strength that she could muster, she looked in the direction where the chief guest was being seated. As the crowd cleared, she had the first glimpse of her role model, Lt. Col. Veer looked dapper in a blue blazer, and he wore a matching designer scarf around his collar. He looked incredibly fit and handsome and never a day above thirty years in age. He was no less than what she had anticipated, even better. She looked at Sunita, who, hiding from Bhumi's father sitting beside her, gestured her positive ideas about the man.

She had to come to senses when the compère called her to begin her recital.

And she had to fight with all her guts to complete her composition. She didn't know how she had fared, her mind was numb. Maybe her performance was ok because she received great ovation, even the poets sitting on stage looked impressed. Few even came up to her to congratulate. Father and Sunita looked super excited too. She was in a different world all the time and hadn't looked towards him even once during her whole recital.

For the chief guest, he too seemed impressed with the young poetess. Maybe because he could relate to her writings, they were similar to his own. This girl, whoever she was, has got a bright future ahead, he thought. She was extremely beautiful and had a great voice, a great combination.

At the end of the session, as Col. Veer politely gestured for the permission to leave, he was asked to facilitate the young participants. The compère announced,

"Now I would like to ask the chief guest to please come onto the stage and distribute some prizes to the participants.

The 'Most promising poet' award for today's performance goes to someone who won the hearts of each one of us with her beautiful words. And that poet is, our very own Bhumi."

There was a loud roar of applause. She could see her proud father and Sunita clapping vigorously.

She stepped forward. There he was, Lt. Col. Veer with a memento in his hands. As soon as he heard her name, his facial expressions changed. The girl, his biggest fan, the one he had been avoiding confrontation with even in letters, destiny had suddenly and unexpectedly brought her in front of him.

Bhumi was a bundle of nerves, her cheek turning bright red with the combined effect of shyness and excitement. They glowed further in the flashlight of cameras. She moved forward to receive the award.

He had a deep husky voice.

"Many congratulations. Your words are beautiful, and your voice is even better. A rare combination indeed."

"Thanks,"

It was all that she could manage to say. She was scared that her heart was pounding so loudly that everyone around would sense it.

Suddenly, he whispered,

"If I am not wrong, we know each other."

Bhumi could feel the rising hair on the nap her neck.

She picked up her gaze and looking directly into his deep eyes, said,

"Only the fortunate ones get their replies. Thanks for

recognising me."

With those words, she collected her award, turned and hurriedly left the stage.

His gaze followed her till she was lost in the crowd. He managed to get a glimpse of another girl who joined her in the crowd and who was waving excitedly towards him.

As Col. Veer Pratap Singh left for Chakrata, he was intrigued by the beautiful young poetess.

CHAPTER 5

The Rendezvous

Six months later...

Municipal Post Graduate College,

Mussoorie, Uttarakhand.

It's the government degree college that caters to the higher education needs of young boys and girls of not only Mussoorie town, but also to numerous villages scattered among the hills all around. Just outside the town and down the slopes, it is located on Dehradun road. It's a thoroughfare from where one can choose to enter Mussoorie town from its either ends. Roads also lead to some other towns and villages; therefore, it's always abuzz with all kinds of buses and taxis. It indeed is less than a perfect location for an educational institute, and one can easily miss the entrance to the college, but for numerous cycles and motorcycles that are always parked on either side of its gate during the day.

It doesn't look like a college for someone who might be new to the area. But for students, despite it being in depleted condition, it's their gateway to a bright future.

Bhumi and Sunita were the students of the second year of their graduation at the same college. That day, they were sitting on the steps of what was the veranda in front of the classes. The veranda was the common roaming ground for the students, especially when they weren't attending the classes. The girls would sit on the steps that would lead down into the open fields upfront.

Both the friends were talking intently when a group of girls approached them.

One of them got talking.

"Aren't you guys coming on our upcoming college tour?"

She enquired.

"Tour? What tour?"

Sunita chirped.

"Haan, how would you know, you do not have the time, super busy as you always are."

The girl said curtly.

"Yes. We are least interested in these rubbish kind of tours with these jokers."

Sunita said, pointing towards a group of boys who were passing by. One of them turned around and asked angrily,

"Did you say something to us?"

Bhumi got scared, she said hurriedly,

"No, no bhaiya. She was talking to me only."

The boys gave a stern look and began to leave. Bhumi turned to her friend and whispered,

"You will get in big trouble one of these days."

"Why so? Why should they think they are the jokers when there are so many other jokers roaming around, we might be talking about the circus we saw last week?"

Sunita said, refusing to mend her ways. Then turning towards the group of girls who were left speechless by the incident, asked,

"By the way, where you guys are going for the tour?"

"Don't you know? The tour is going to Chakrata this time."

Hearing this, Sunita looked towards Bhumi and rolled her eyes in amazement. This time it was their turn to go speechless.

"What happened, are you girls alright with your mind?"

When a girl enquired, Sunita regained her composure and gesturing towards her friend, said,

"Are you sure, it's Chakrata this time?"

"Why are you so confused? It's only Chakrata, not London. Just like Mussoorie, so boring."

The girl replied.

"If it's Chakrata, then even we can think about joining in. I have heard it's a beautiful place. Isn't it Bhumi?"

Sunita pressed her friend's hand in excitement.

"Let's see."

Bhumi would only say that much. From inside, she still remembered that thumping of her chest on that eventful day. She couldn't keep a count of the sleepless nights and daydreams that had happened to her since that day. When she looked up to Sunita, she found her friend giggling like anything.

Bhumi and Sunita were sitting under the Deodar tree. It was early evening, and the weather was overcast. The Sun was playing hide and seek with passing clouds. Bhumi was trying to write something. Suddenly, she threw her pen away and declared,

"No Suni, I cannot write. That day, I was so anxious; I don't know how and why I said all that to him."

"Never mind. You didn't do anything bad as such. But if you think so, start with an apology …"

"But Suni is it necessary to write at all? He never replies and especially after that horrible incident...I don't think it's a good idea."

"There is nothing wrong in trying, dear. Now we know that he is posted at Chakrata and with our college tour happening, we must explore the possibilities. I think even Lord Shiva wants us to do that."

"Even I want to meet…Just once, but…I don't know why I am scared, Suni?"

"Don't you hesitate Bhumi, just try once; if he is not interested, then put it to rest once and for all. At least, you will be relieved knowing that you tried."

Pushed by her friend, Bhumi began to write a letter to Lt.Col.Veer-

"I would like to say sorry for my behaviour on that day. I shouldn't have said that. Even Sunita believes the same. I was immersed in such feelings that I wasn't able to control my emotions. I was too scared perhaps, not even in my wildest dreams I ever expected to meet you like that. I hope you will understand.

I want to meet you once; I have been your fan for a very long time. Next to next Sunday, our college tour is coming to Chakrata. Suni says I must meet you once. Maybe, you will be able to spare a few minutes to meet us.

Unable to insist, I can only hope to get a reply this time. Otherwise, I will realise that our meeting on that day was our first and last meeting of this lifetime.

Bhumi.

Lt. Col. Singh was leaving for home from his office when he received the letter. The Sahayak handed him the envelope as he was getting up from his chair. He immediately recognised it by the writing on the envelope. He stopped in his movements and began to read the letter.

It was evening time. The monsoon had already set in. As he finished reading the words of his biggest fan, he looked out of his office window. Anticipating the early rains, the sky was full of mountain birds flying back to their dwellings. It had been overcast throughout the day. Now, as the evening approached, the Sun had broken free from the stranglehold of dense clouds, and the horizon was brilliantly coloured with the rays of setting Sun; a million colours danced through the evening sky.

It was providing a definite brightness to that rather dull evening landscape. Veer looked towards the horizon for a very long time, he was contemplating deeply. Loneliness had always been his constant companion since a very early age, but today it was hurting like never before. That loneliness had made him a recluse, a man of few spoken words but the one who would fly on a piece of paper. Perhaps it was because his work and his writing were his only respite. But sometimes, nothing would work to make him feel better. He thought it was one such moment.

Suddenly, he picked up a pen and scribbled something on a piece of paper. He then took the paper along with the letter and left for home.

Sunita was sitting on the roof of her house when she saw Bhumi rushing through the flight of stairs.

'Mind your steps beta,' she could hear the voice of her mother coming from below. It was directed towards her friend, she knew. By the time Bhumi came closer, she was out of her breath. She grabbed Sunita with excitement, who was thrown off balance by the sudden attack.

"Have you gone mad Bhumi?"

She shouted.

"Just leave me, will you?"

"First guess why am I so happy."

Bhumi demanded.

"I know very well."

"Really? Then tell."

"Your Papa has divorced that lady who is your stepmother."

"Stop the nonsense. It's never going to happen."

"Then, you have got your marriage fixed."

"Never again."

"Then I don't know. When madam is angry, I am the one who is in trouble. Now that madam is happy, again I have to bear the brunt. This is too much."

Sunita feigned anger.

"Don't you try to be melodramatic? I will tell you. Listen, you were right, Suni. You were so, so right. I got a reply from him after so many years."

She was beaming with delight as she said that.

"What? Come again."

Even Sunita was startled.

"Yes, that's right, darling. I have got a reply, see."

She was holding a piece of paper.

Sunita snatched it from her hands. The paper was torn into two pieces. Sunita could only get the plain piece of paper; the written one was still in Bhumi's hands.

"Show me what he has written, would you?"

She pleaded.

"Only this much."

She showed her the contents on the paper. It read,

'CALL ME ON THIS NUMBER ON THAT DAY!'

There was a phone number written below it.

"That's it?"

Sunita enquired.

"Ya, that's all."

She replied.

"What a miser this army man is!"

Sunita declared.

"You don't know, the poets would never use two words when one will do."

Bhumi tried to defend him.

"Ya, you are right. You are the poetess, he is the poet. Who are we? We are nothing, haan!"

Teasing her, Sunita murmured in a dejected tone.

Both the friends burst into laughter. Sunita felt so good for her best friend. She deserved such moments of happiness, she thought. For Bhumi, if not best, it certainly was one of the better days of her young life.

Chhavni Bazaar.

Chakrata, Uttarakhand.

The college tour had just reached Chakrata. Guided by the fat lady teacher, all the students were getting down from the tour bus. Dressed elegantly in the traditional attire of 'Salwar Suit,' Bhumi and Sunita were also a part of it. Bhumi was wearing a pink coloured suit, the reflection of which glowed on her cheeks, and she looked stunning. She was no doubt the most elegant among the crowd of college girls.

The Chhavni bazaar is a typical military Cantonment market catering to the needs of mostly the army men when the rather small army CSD Canteen is unable to fulfil their needs. At Chakrata, the market possesses that particular trait of hills, the road going up and down the terrain, small wooden shops selling items of daily needs, and the lazy elegance of shopkeepers and customers alike, where nobody seems to be in any hurry and time moves at rather a slow pace. A lot of shops sold famous Rajma and other pulses that are traditionally grown on the beautiful terrace fields all around the Jaunsar hills.

The students were walking through the bazaar. Both Bhumi and Sunita were looking for something among the line of shops on either side of the road. Everyone was chirping, and the lady teacher was finding it challenging to bring semblance to the loud group. After walking for a while, both the friends found what they were looking for; it was a public telephone booth that was coloured with bright yellow paint. Bhumi gestured towards Sunita.

Sunita stopped and waited for the teacher. Because of her overweight, she was trying hard to keep pace with the young girls. Walking beside the teacher for a while, Sunita said to her,

"Ma'am, Bhumi wants to make a call to her paternal aunt. She lives here only."

"Here? Where?"

She was suspicious as most teachers are.

"Her husband, I mean Bhumi's uncle is an army officer. He is posted here."

Sunita replied confidently. By this time, Bhumi too had started walking beside her. Hearing Sunita calling him as an 'uncle' again, she pulled her hair from behind.

"Ouch!"

Sunita cried.

"What happened?"

The teacher demanded.

"Nothing, ma'am. It will hardly take few minutes."

Bhumi said hurriedly.

"Okay. We all are collecting there. You both should come back as soon as possible. Understand?"

Gesturing towards a point at a distance where all the girls were getting together, the teacher demanded.

Both friends clinched their fists in excitement as they turned and moved away from the teacher.

Nestled between Tons and Yamuna river, Chakrata again is a Cantonment town in district Dehradun. It was a part of combined Uttar Pradesh until the 21st century. Today, Dehradun is the state capital of Uttarakhand. At the beginning of the 20th century, it was all part of the 'United Province' under the British.

Chakrata is located seventy-three kilometers east of Mussoorie. Its Cantonment was established by one Col. Hume of 55th Regiment of British Indian Army. Today, it is the permanent garrison of the secretive and elite 'Special Frontier Force' or the 'SFF', also known as 'Establishment two-two'- the only Tibetan unit in the Indian Army that was raised after Indo-China war of 1962.

Today, SFF is a part of 'Research and Analysis Wing' or simply 'RAW,' the Indian equivalent of American secret service, the CIA. The RAW imparts weapons and survival training to elite soldiers here. There are six battalions stationed at Chakrata, and each one of them is headed by its Commanding Officer, the CO.

The rank of the CO is generally Lt. Col or the Colonel.

In the summers of 1992, Lt. Col. Veer Pratap Singh was posted on deputation at Chakrata. He was in his office when the army telephone exchange connected the call.

"There is a call for you, Saheb."

The operator was saying.

"Get it through."

The Lt. Col. replied and waited patiently. There were a

few 'clicks' to be heard on the line as the connections were established.

"Sir?"

There she was, on the other side of the line.

"Yes."

For Bhumi, standing anxiously in a public telephone booth a few miles away, it was unmistakably the same deep husky voice. Though Sunita was huddled close to her, she shivered with nervous energy. Her heart thumped so loudly, she was sure even Sunita would hear it.

Mustering all her courage, she softly murmured,

"It's me. Bhumi."

"Nice to hear your voice again, Bhumi. How are you?"

She felt his deep voice was coming from far off distance. There was something in that voice that always filled her with tons of nervous energy. It was not in her control.

"I am good. How are you?"

She was sweet and polite, he thought. There was something in the girl's voice that made him want to hear her more and more. Surely he hasn't forgotten her recital on the stage on that fateful day.

"Very good. So you are here in Chakrata?"

He was asking. Sunita was making a lot of gestures; Bhumi found it challenging to concentrate, she was contributing to her nervousness in a big way.

"Yes, we came today only."

"Great. So you wanted to meet me."

She was relieved that he asked for that.

"Yes."

Ignoring Sunita's promptings, she said in a shallow voice. No matter how close her friend might be to her, some feelings couldn't be shared.

"So where are you right now and what your programs are?"

He asked. He didn't look like a man who would talk much, she thought. On his part, it pained him to act so businesslike.

"We are gathering for lunch now. We will go to Gulaab Singh Degree College then. Maybe we will be free by three or four o'clock from there."

She sounded a bit confused, or maybe she is too nervous. He was thinking.

"Where are you exactly?"

He asked again.

"Oh! We are…"

She tried hard to read Sunita's lips. She was never good with the names and maps. Then she managed to say,

"We are in Chhavni bazaar…"

She felt silent.

"Okay. At four O'clock, there will be an army's gypsy stationed outside the college gate. Havildar Jai Singh is the name of the driver. He is my man. He will bring you here, you can trust him. Is this fine with you?"

Bhumi panicked and looked towards her friend. She was moving her head in affirmation. Also, his voice was so authoritative, it was almost impossible to deny.

"Okay... Sir."

Was all she managed to say in the end.

"See you in the evening then."

The line went silent. Bhumi regained her ability to hear the voices around. Everything was normal and the business around the market was moving as usual. But Bhumi felt differently.

"The deal is struck but my friend is stuck!" , Sunita said smilingly.

Bhumi took her friend's hand and placing it over her heart said, "Look, I am about to get a heart attack and you are trying to act funny."

"Never mind. Your heart will be taken care of shortly."

She refused to budge.

"It is good that you will be coming along at least."

"Me? No way."

"Please Sunita. I won't go without you", Bhumi was begging.

"I won't come."

"You are my best friend, don't you forget that."

"That's why, precisely."

"How would you explain that?"

"Darling, if I come along with you, who will manage that fat lady?"

Sunita gestured towards their teacher. Oblivious of everything and everyone, she was eating the *golgappas* from a roadside vendor with great intent.

"What if he turns out to be a criminal?" She tried one last time.

"Don't try to be dramatic. He is a respected army officer. Maybe he will make you meet his family. There might be a lovely wife and some small kids who would call you 'mausi' if you happen to win over them."

Sunita teased. But suddenly, the possibilities dawned upon Bhumi. What if Suni was right, she hasn't thought it that way. It was true that she knew nothing about the personal life of the elusive poet. She turned serious, even sad. Sensing the same, Sunita tried to change the topic and cried, "But this all can happen only if that fatty would allow you to go. So watch my magic."

Without waiting for a reply, she swiftly went ahead to confront the teacher.

The teacher had her mouth full, the *golgappas* were big, and she was having a hard time gulping them down when Sunita attacked.

"Ma'am, Bhumi's aunt wants to meet her. She has got something for her mother to give."

"Okay. She can come."

The teacher spoke as clearly as she could with her mouth full. Bhumi fought hard to suppress her laugh. She turned her face away from the teacher. But Sunita miraculously managed to keep a straight face.

"Ma'am, she is a big officer's wife."

Sunita protested.

"If she is that big, she should remain home."

The teacher said curtly as she gulped down another one. She was still eyeing more *golgappas.*

"Exactly ma'am, but it's only because she can't walk. She is sick. But she is so generous and fond of distributing gifts to one and all. She was telling Bhumi that she even has got a gift for you. She is very kind."

The teacher stopped eating. She looked confused.

"But you girls are my responsibility here. I can't permit it," She protested.

"What about the gifts, ma'am. She will have to give them to others. Let it be, then ma'am."

Sunita turned to leave.

"If it's that important, then I should permit, *na.*"

The teacher suddenly murmured behind her back. She couldn't see the girls smiling.

The teacher said, "Bhumi, you can go after visiting the college. And you should come back straight to the hotel as soon as possible. Do you know the hotel? And how will you go?"

"Ma'am, her aunt is sending an army car to fetch and drop her. The gifts seem quite big *na?*" Sunita said hurriedly.

It was the onset of the rainy season, there were clouds in the sky, and they played hide and seek with the Sun. Bhumi hid behind her friend, she was holding her hands tightly as both the girls walked away happily.

It was Lt. Col. Veer's official residence. The garden in front of the house was very well managed. It was the first thing that caught Bhumi's gaze as the car approached the house. It was her maiden trip chaffered in any vehicle. In fact, a lot many new things were happening in her life these days, causing new feelings to emerge within her heart. She felt excited and nervous as the vehicle stopped in front of the porch.

She caught the first glimpse of the handsome army man; he was standing at the door. He looked smart, even boyish in his casual jeans and t-shirt.

"Good evening Bhumi. Please come."

He came forward to welcome her.

"Good evening, Sir."

She was a bit hesitant. He opened the door for her. Once inside, he offered her a seat. Bhumi looked around. The décor was simple yet elegant. There were lots of books and pictures all over the place. There were army artifacts belonging to different places he had been stationed over the years. There was a wooden stand at a corner where many caps and hats were hanging; most of them looked to be a part of some army uniform. On the far wall, some trophies and medallions were decorated, that was a testimony of his brilliant career. Everything bore a simple look; even the furniture was plain yet functional.

He let her soak in the atmosphere. The 'sahayak' brought a glass of water.

"What would you like to have- tea or coffee?" He was asking.

"Nothing...Sir. It's ok."

"No, it's not done. You will have to take something."

He insisted. She was confused, she fell silent.

Sensing her dilemma, he proposed, "It's alright. Are you comfortable with coffee?"

The same deep voice. It was difficult to deny.

"Okay. "

She doesn't speak much, he thought.

Bhumi looked around.

"Who else is there in your family?" She asked.

"Oh, you are asking about my wife and...."

He felt silent for a while. Then he regained his composure and smiled.

"I do not have parents anymore. As for my wife, she doesn't live with me these days. We are separated."

He said as a matter of fact.

"Oh! I am sorry."

She could feel a certain kind of relief within her as he said that. Perhaps what Sunita had said in the afternoon was still there at the back of her mind. She was expecting a house full of kids.

"No, it's alright. I am used to be on my own. It helps in my writings as well."

He replied as her mind processed the new information about his wife and family.

"How about your family, Bhumi?"

He asked.

"My father is a school teacher. My mother died when I was small, though I still remember her. I have a stepmother and two small brothers and sisters."

He could sense how she turned serious, even sad as she said that. Maybe she still missed her mother. He was aware her life was not all that rosy while growing up as a kid. He remembered her letters, and it showed in her writings too. He was a poet, and he could relate to her in more ways than one.

The coffee was served. The sky was getting dense outside. On the inside, Bhumi's mind was flooded by the clouds of emotions. Overcoming the same, she suddenly said,

"Can I ask you something?"

"Yes, sure."

One could easily believe that voice.

"Did you receive the letters that I used to write to you?"

"Yes. Regularly. Why do you ask that?"

"Because you never replied to any of those."

He left his place, went to a drawer, and brought a file back. Passing on the same to her, he replied,

"It contains all the letters written by you till date. I never replied because I did not have answers to your questions. Even I had my own unanswered questions all the time. We both have been busy fighting our own battles, Bhumi. You have been my most loyal fan. But believe me; you were never away from my thoughts and in my prayers."

Her heart banged against her chest, and she began to go through all her letters kept meticulously in the folder. Suddenly, a gust of wind came through the window blowing some of the letters away and on to the floor. The mountain wind was damp. It carried a lot of rain, and Veer could sense that.

She was trying to collect the letters from the floor. He tried to help her, and it brought them closer than ever before. She smelled beautiful. She began to feel awkward, and suddenly she said, "I think I shall make a move now. The weather looks bad."

She looked outside. They both went silent for a while. If silence would be a language, they spoke a lot.

Finally, he said, "Let me drop you back then."

Mustering all of her courage, she looked directly into his deep eyes and replied,

"I will manage. I have to find my own ways."

For the first time, Veer noticed that the colour of her eyes was unique. It was a different kind of brown, a bright sparkly brown. Her eyes were moist like those of a kid, and they possessed the same innocence. If eyes were the windows to the soul, this girl had a beautiful soul, he thought.

For Bhumi, that man was as handsome as she had ever seen in her young life. He looked caring, passionate, serious, and responsible. How a woman could deny such a man, she thought about his wife.

"No, this is not done. I will drop you as I am free."

She regained her composure when she heard him say that. It was almost impossible to deny the man. When they came out, the driver was standing by the side of the vehicle.

Seeing his officer, he came to attention.

Veer ordered,

"I am going to drive the vehicle, Jai Singh. You won't be needed again today, so you may leave."

"*Ji Saheb.*"

The driver said and opened the door of the vehicle for his boss.

As they both took their seats inside, there was a thunder in the clouds. It made her shudder. Lt. Col. Veer turned to his orderly and said,

"The weather looks bad. Even you can leave, Negi. I will call you when I need to."

"Jee, Sir."

The 'sahayak' said obediently and saluted their officer.

As they left, the first droplets of monsoon rains began to hit the windscreen of the army vehicle.

Chakrata is a small town. She told him the name of the hotel where they were going to put up for the night. They drove through the quiet circular roads of the Cantonment. The wind was strong, and the rain got heavier as they moved forward. In the mountains of the north, it rains quite a lot during monsoons. Many times, it goes on incessantly for days without a break. The clouds would bring water and hitting the nearby mountains, pour it down with great vigor.

As the rain got heavier, the rather small rain wipers of the army Gypsy couldn't keep the windscreen clear. Veer slowed down the speed to keep it under control while managing the depleted visibility. Bhumi was quiet, words failed to come to her lips. She wanted to speak a lot; she had thought of asking so much, but when the moment came, her mind was blank. She was aware that it could be the last meeting between them. With pouring emotions that could easily match the rains outside, she kept on gazing in front, although there was hardly anything visible outside other than the falling heavens.

It took fifteen minutes to cover what would usually be a five-minute drive. When they finally reached there, the hotel bore a forlorn look. The group of college girls was nowhere to be seen. The reception was empty but for a lone receptionist. The rain was hitting the window panes, and the tin roof above made great noises.

"The weather turned so bad. No one has reported yet, maybe they are stuck somewhere."

The receptionist informed. They waited. Ten minutes

passed.

Bhumi turned to him and said,

"I will wait here; it might be sometime before my group arrives. Thank you so much."

He looked into her eyes. She looked scared.

"In this weather and under these circumstances, it's not a good idea for you to wait here."

He said, and without waiting for a reply, he took out a pen and scribbled a phone number on a piece of paper. Passing the same to the receptionist, he said,

"When the group is here, give this number to their in charge. Ask her to call on this number."

"Now come on, Bhumi. Let's go, we will come again. You are shivering."

Taking her by the elbow, he let her out and made her climb the vehicle, protecting her from rain showers all the time.

Bhumi was spellbound. For some reason, she couldn't utter a word. She felt good that she will spend some more time with him. She will talk this time, she thought.

When they reached back, she was shivering with the combined effect of excitement and cold weather. High above, the thunderstorms now accompanied the falling rains. As soon as the vehicle stopped, he took off his jacket and coming to her side, put it on her shoulders to save her from getting drenched. This was the second moment in half an hour when he could smell her, and she could feel his warmth.

As he was opening the front door of the house, a majestic thunderstorm accompanied the lightning, and as a reflex action, she turned and hid her head against his chest. She was so scared of lightening since her childhood.

It all happened so instantly, even Veer couldn't think of anything. He put an arm around her and took her inside the house. Once inside and in a safe environ, she realized the awkwardness of the situation. Apart from being in her father's arms as a child, she had never felt so safe in a long time. Her heart did not want to part, but her mind was telling her to get away from the warmth and security his closeness had created for her. Even he seemed to possess no intention of letting her go in a hurry.

The man she had been secretly admiring since her teenage days was holding her in his arms. She found it impossible to move. He took her to the sofa and made her sit there gently.

"It's alright. It was just a thunderstorm."

He softly said.

He moved authoritatively and brought an electric room heater and placed it close to her. Massive hailstones had started falling outside; they were hitting and bouncing off the window panes.

"I will get you something warm to drink, you are cold."

He said as he moved to the kitchen. Bhumi looked outside; she had rarely seen such kind of rains. The wind was very strong, it was a hailstorm. She picked up the file from the table, it was still there. As she flipped through her own letters, it became apparent that he had kept each one of them safe. Going through her writings of the early years, she felt awkward. They were so childish. The old memories came flooding.

The ringing of the telephone bell brought her back

from her reveries. She looked around; maybe he was still in the kitchen. She had lost the count of time. Hesitantly, she picked up the phone. Sunita was on the line, and she was sputtering.

"Bhumi, where are you? Thank God you are safe at your *mausi's* place."

Bhumi told her that she had been to the hotel earlier.

"Ya, we were told by the receptionist, he gave this phone number to ma'am. Maybe 'uncle' gave it to him. You know, how bad we got stuck, we somehow managed to reach just now. It's been hailstorm outside; so many trees have fallen on the roads."

She did not allow Bhumi to speak. She was babbling.

"Ya, ma'am is here only. No, you won't be able to come, *na*. The road is blocked. What about the gifts? Oh, they are heavy. Achha, there are dry fruits, as well. You do one thing, Bhumi, come first thing in the morning. 'Uncle' will drop you. And don't forget the gifts. I will tell ma'am, she will understand everything."

"But…Suni,"

Sunita wasn't listening.

"It's ok with ma'am Bhumi. She says you shouldn't take the risk. It's not your fault, how could you wait alone at the hotel? Uncle did the right thing. Say my hello to him, would you?"

Sunita was teasing her.

"Sure, I will. You will have to repent for this Suni."

She murmured. Sunita disconnected the line.

He was back with coffee.

"Who was there on the phone? He enquired.

"It was Sunita."

"What was she saying?"

"She said ma'am was saying that I shouldn't try to come in this weather. It is a big storm even the roads are blocked. But I think I should go."

"I am afraid it's not possible at the moment. Even I got a call that a heavy tree has fallen close to our gate. They will try to remove it, but it will take time."

Passing on the coffee to her, he went close to the window.

"The rain Gods are still not repenting."

He said, looking out to the falling rains. He came back and sat on the opposite sofa. She looked disturbed.

"Do not worry. I have asked them to intimate me as soon as the roadblock gets cleared."

He tried to assure her.

She couldn't say anything at once. Unable to find words, she picked up a book from the side table. It was the latest collection of poems by him. Flipping through its pages, she asked, "Is it your new collection?"

"Ya, it was published only recently. And one of the ghazals is being sung in a movie as well."

He was casual as if it was no big deal.

"Would you like to hear that song?" Suddenly he asked.

"Really? Ya sure, I would love to."

Bhumi got really excited. For once, she forgot about the rain or where she was and under what circumstances.

He smiled and moved to the mantle place where the music system was placed. He fiddled with the compact discs for a while; they were the new gadgets in the market. As the sound of music started filling the room, the outside voices of rain and wind died down. For once, there was no sign of storm in that cozy room. He came back; she showed him the book and asked,

"Which among these is the ghazal being played on the system?"

He came and sitting beside her, showed her the exact one from the book. Then he said,

"There is one more important thing about this particular ghazal. If you listen to it carefully, you will realize that it fits beautifully to the present situation that we are in right now."

In the background, the melodious voice of the singer began to fill the spaces-

'Kaise Jaoge Ye Barsaat Na Jaane Degi.
'Dil Mein Jo Baat Hai Wo Baat Na Jaane Degi.

'You won't be able to go in the rain; the weather wouldn't allow you to,

You won't be able to follow your brain; the heart wouldn't allow you to.'

She closed her eyes and tried hard to concentrate on the verses. He was right, they conveyed her exact feelings. How did he know in advance about what was happening to her right now? Her breath turned heavy. As she put her hand on the sofa, she suddenly felt his hands coming over hers. They were warm and gentle, and so were his words coming out of speakers. She kept her eyes closed as if she was dreaming.

The song continued in the background…

भीगा मौसम है, हवाओं पे रंग बिखरा है।

Bheega mausam hai hawaon pe rang bikhra hai.

तुमको पा लेने का अरमान दिल में निखरा है।

Tumko paa lene ka armaan dil mein nikhra hai.

महके जज़्बात की ये रात न जाने देगी।

Mehke jazbaat ki ye raat na jaane degi.

कैसे जाओगे ये बरसात न जाने देगी।

Kaise jaoge ye barsaat na jaane degi.

He took her gently in his arms; she allowed herself to be swayed over and slowly rested her head on his chest.

सुर्ख होठों पे थिरकती हैं दहकती बूंदें।

Surkh hoton pe thirakti hain dahakti boondein.

भीगी ज़ुल्फ़ों में सरकती हैं बहकती बूंदें।

Bheegi zulfon mein sarakti hain bahakti boondein.

महके लम्हों की ये सौगात न जाने देगी।

Mehke lamhon ki ye saugaat na jaane degi.

कैसे जाओगे ये बरसात न जाने देगी।

Kaise jaoge ye barsaat na jaane degi.

He began to play with her hair, trying to untangle the curls. He touched her lips gently with his thumb, wiping away the droplets of water resting over their lusciousness.

तेज़ तूंफां ने बहा रखा है देखो हमको।

Tez toonfa ne bahaa rakhaa hai dekho humko.

दिल के अरमाँ ने ज़ला रखा है देखो हमको।

Dil ke armaa ne jalaa rakha hai dekho humko.

भीगे जज़्बात की ये रात न जाने देगी।

Bheege jazbaat ki ye raat na jaane degi.

कैसे जाओगे ये बरसात न जाने देगी।

Kaise jaoge ye barsaat na jaane degi.

She tightly pressed her face against his chest. He soaked in her fragrance and holding her beautiful face with both of his hands, he pulled her close. As he pressed his lips against hers, she closed her eyes.

बहके अरमानों के संवर जाने की शाम आयी है।

Behke armano ke sanwar jaane ki shaam aayi hai.

महके अहसासों के निखर जाने की शाम आयी है।

Mehke ahsaaso ke nikhar jaane ki shaam aayi hai.

भीगे जज़्बात की ये सौगात न जाने देगी।

Bheege jazbaat ki ye saugaat na jaane degi.

कैसे जाओगे ये बरसात न जाने देगी।

Kaise jaoge ye barsaat na jaane degi.

Slowly he let her lie down onto the couch. She shifted to make space for him, he could only adjust sideways. With his right leg over hers, he rested his upper body onto his left elbow and looked lovingly into her eyes. Unable to hold the gaze, she pressed him close to her. He began to kiss behind her ears and then, on her tender neck.

शाम गहराई है और रात हुई जाती है।

Shaam gahrai hai aur raat hui jaati hai.

ज़िस्म से रूह की मुलाक़ात हुई जाती है।

Zism se ruh ki mulaqaat hui jaati hai.

सुबह से पहले की ये रात ना जाने देगी।

Subeh se pahle ki ye raat na jaane degi.

कैसे जाओगे ये बरसात न जाने देगी।

Kaise jaoge ye barsaat na jaane degi.

Her face shone with the mixed feelings of little pain and much pleasure.

The night had fallen, but the storm was still going strong. Inside, the light burned brightly and so did both of them.

CHAPTER 6

The Journey And The Transformation

If a single night could change someone's life upside down, it changed Bhumi's. The girl who came on a college trip was not the same when she returned to her hometown the next day. Everything had changed for her. Lt. Col. Veer became the most important person in her life. She was already an introvert, a daydreamer. Now she became even quieter. He had promised her a life of togetherness, and she constantly dreamt about it. For the first time in her life, she didn't divulge much about her personal experiences with Sunita. It wasn't that she didn't want to tell, it was only that she somehow felt uncomfortable explaining everything to her. Even Sunita did not force her much. She could know a lot without being told, and she seemed calm about what she knew. She was that close.

A month passed. Veer was transferred to New Delhi and was attached to the Research and Analysis Wing, the parent body of SFF. He had written to her that some important postings were in the offing, and he was trying to find a way. The letter was delivered by someone when she was on her way to college. She lost the count of the number of times she had read that letter.

By the end of the month, Bhumi missed her menstrual date. She waited for a few weeks and then, unable to contain her anxiety, mustered all her courage to visit an unassuming lady doctor. A simple test confirmed her fears, she was pregnant. It was another secret she couldn't share with anyone, not even Sunita. She was in a state of shock for the next several days. She tried to read as much as she could about the pregnancy, without raising the alarm. And she became scared to death.

By the end of the week, she decided that the situation was urgent enough to use the solitary phone number that belonged to New Delhi.

Bhumi chose a public telephone booth that was far away from her home. It was at the library, the other end of Mall Road. He had instructed her to use the number in case of extreme emergency only. With shaky fingers, she dialled the number. At least the line was connected on the first try. She waited nervously as the bell kept ringing. Within that short span of time, a thousand fearful thoughts came to her mind. What if he fails to pick up the phone? Maybe he has been transferred again since then. Perhaps he was out of town. Of course, she would come again but if he doesn't pick up the phone today, tomorrow and the day after?

As she was losing hope and feeling panicky, suddenly the phone was picked up at the last bell.

"Hello, Bhumi!"

It was the same deep husky voice. She felt as if her life returned. Her voice choked with emotions.

"How did you know it's me, Veer?" She managed to say.

"Because nobody else would call me on this number."

His tone was obvious. For the first time since the news of her pregnancy, she began to feel confident again. His voice was so reassuring.

"But you sound disturbed Bhumi. Is everything alright?"

He asked with a genuine hint of concern in his voice. She was relieved that he could sense her fears.

"I have to tell you something very important."

"What is it, Bhumi?"

"Veer….," She hesitated.

"Come on, go ahead."

"I am pregnant."

She blurted out suddenly.

"What?"

Now it was his turn to be surprised. Then, regaining his composure, he asked,

"Are you sure Bhumi?"

"I missed my date. I saw a doctor and she confirmed."

Her voice was concerned, even fearful. The next few moments felt like an eternity. She got impatient,

"What shall I do Veer? I am so scared."

Her voice cracked with fear.

"Don't worry Bhumi. Everything will be alright."

He said and then added,

"Just give me one day to sort it out. Call me tomorrow on this number. Same time. I will make everything fine. Trust me."

"I have no other option, Veer. I will call you tomorrow."

She put the receiver down and felt a shiver that ran down her spine.

Bhumi could not sleep well that night. Her stepmother had given her some cumbersome tasks in the evening that she was scared to do. Hiding from everyone's gaze, she had kept on looking at her belly. It looked like growing all the time. She couldn't do anything about that. Her stepmother was even disrespectful towards her father. She wouldn't understand why father would bear her all the time. He seemed to have lost his capacity to object even to her bizarre theatrics. She felt pity for her father.

Sunita had always been her last hope. Now even she had started complaining about her indifferent attitude these days. Her only solace was that Veer appeared genuinely concerned on the phone. She felt relieved for a while. But as she hit the bed at night, fear once again gripped her. Even after reassuring herself, again and again, fear and doubt refused to get out of her thoughts. What could he do after all, especially from that distance? The signs of pregnancy would become more and more apparent with time. What solution could he have for this? And it was not a problem for her. She could already feel a life inside her womb. It was a gift of love, from the best man she had ever known.

It was well past midnight when she really went to sleep. She had a dream that night. That she was playing in an exotic garden with a beautiful kid. She didn't know whether it was a baby boy or girl, it was just a beautiful kid. She was trying to catch butterflies in the garden and the kid giggled with the failure of her each effort. Every time she would get close to the brilliantly coloured butterfly, it would fly away. The kid would giggle more and more, she fell in love with the baby. Then she fell out of the dream and into a deep slumber.

It was a few minutes to five in the evening when Bhumi entered the public telephone booth the next day. She gestured towards the shopkeeper who also owned the grocery shop just beyond the booth. She closed the door carefully behind her and dialled the phone number that she now remembered by heart.

She was again surprised when he picked up the phone on the very first bell. Sure he was eagerly waiting for her call.

"Hello, Bhumi!"

Her heart sank once again. There was something in that deep voice that never failed to increase her heartbeat.

"Hello!" She replied.

"How are you?" He asked.

"I am good." She replied.

He could feel that she was tense, very tense, in fact.

"May I ask you something, Bhumi?"

"Yes," She said obediently.

"Would you…."

He showed a rare hesitation.

"I mean… what would you like to do?"

She was confused,

"I do not understand," She said.

"Do... with the baby Bhumi."

He finally managed to say. She felt silent as she did not know how to respond.

"Please tell me. Only then I would be able to make some decision."

He pleaded. He looked desperate, on the brink of making a final call.

"I want our baby, Veer."

Mustering all the courage at her disposal, she was almost requesting.

"Are you sure?" He reconfirmed.

"This baby belongs to both of us. Will always remind us of the beautiful moments that we spent together. Also, I cannot kill an innocent life."

She fell silent again.

"Me too, Bhumi."

He seemed honest as he said that. A smile dawned on her lips.

"Okay. Then listen to me very carefully."

Suddenly, his voice turned serious.

"I have given it a lot of thought since yesterday. And there seems to be only one solution at the moment. But it would demand some bold steps from both of us. Are you ready for that, Bhumi?"

"I can do anything to be with you and have my baby, Veer."

She had also been thinking all the time. She was getting increasingly impatient to hear what was there in his mind. Her life depended on that.

"Can you leave your house to live with me?"

And then he added, "Forever."

Tears rolled down Bhumi's eyes as a sudden burst of emotions engulfed her whole being. In that one moment, a thousand thoughts crossed her already overburdened brain. All humiliations at the hands of her stepmother, the passing away of her mother, the guilt, the helplessness of her father, everything went through her memory like a bullet train. The bruised and beaten face of her father hung like a portrait just in front of her eyes. With blurred eyes, she could see herself sitting in her father's lap as a kid. He would hold her in his arms; she etched with the desire of getting into those safe arms again.

Overwhelmed by emotions, she sobbed silently. Being a writer, he was capable of feeling her pain.

"I know what you are going through Bhumi. But trust me, this is the only way. And I promise to keep you by my side, always!"

She heard his voice as if it was coming from some faraway place. She believed him, he was so much like her. Was there anyone who would miss her if she was gone, except her father? He would survive too, she was sure. Having succumbed to his second wife, with her stepbrother and sister, he now had a family to look after and share his life with. It would keep him more than busy.

There was a long silence.

"Bhumi, are you there?" He asked.

"Haan."

Coming out of her thoughts, she replied.

"Are you comfortable with the idea of spending rest of your life with me?"

He tried to lighten up the environment. She felt it was in continuation of the dream that she had last night. Perhaps he was the butterfly she had been chasing all through her teenage years. She felt a sudden urge to scream.

"Yes, yes, I would love to. I have been waiting all my life for this."

Instead, she softly said, "Jee!"

"Then listen to me carefully."

His voice was serious again.

"Three days from now, on coming Monday, you will have to reach the Bandstand at 11 in the morning. Do you know where the Bandstand is?"

"Yes, I know. I live here."

He smiled. She hadn't lost her sense of humour even under such circumstances, he thought.

"Good. In the taxi parking there, you will find a white Ambassador with the registration number- DLE 0533. You will ask the driver's name, his name is Sukhdev Singh. He is assigned with the task of bringing you safely to me. You can trust him."

"Do you have a pen and paper, Bhumi?"

It was the voice of a man who knew what he was doing. It was difficult not to trust that voice.

"Yes, I have got it."

She noted down all important details.

"One more thing Bhumi, before you reach home, remember everything by heart and destroy the paper. This is important for your safety. Behave normally for the next three days. Do not tell anybody and don't carry anything except what is most necessary, like your educational and other documents. You will get everything else here."

He seemed to have planned everything meticulously. It felt good that she was the most important person in his life at the moment.

Bhumi returned home, filled with all kinds of emotions. For the next two days, she tried to spend as much time with her father as she could, without looking suspicious. Again and again, she tried to reassure herself that everything would be alright with the passage of time and soon she would be able to introduce Veer to father. He will definitely like him, how could one refuse someone so calm and gentle. She took care of her plants like never before, tending to them when she wasn't with Sunita or father. Surprisingly, the tantrums and scolding of her stepmother didn't affect her the way they used to.

She did a little packing on Sunday night, after everyone went to sleep. Along with a few pairs of clothes, she put her personal diary and the pen given by her father on her last birthday. She was used to noting down everything in that diary on daily basis at the end of day, she didn't even miss it on that day as well. She kept her collection of writings and the small statue of Lord Shiva presented by Sunita.

As she hit the bed, she thought about Sunita. Just last week someone had come to her house with a marriage proposal. The boy was a govt. servant and Sunita's marriage was fixed. It was to take place at the end of the year, in December. Both friends had cried in seclusion in the vicinity of the Deodar tree that day. The childhood friends were going to part, she didn't know how she would survive without Sunita. She had always been her last resort. She had repeatedly asked Lord Shiva, her favourite God, that why her only friend was being snatched away from her. Just before falling to sleep, she felt like she knew the answer.

'Because God wanted her to attend Sunita's wedding with Veer, the love of her life.' She thought.

Sunita would prove to be a great sister in law, she was sure!

The next several days proved to the best days of Bhumi's life. All her fears and apprehensions proved to be unfounded. When she had reached the taxi stand, the atmosphere was like that of a commotion. There were hordes of tourists all around, many of them leaving after spending the weekend at the queen of hills that Mussoorie was. If there was any chance of someone recognising her and see her leave in a taxi, it was further dimmed by the presence of that kind of crowd.

He had chosen the time wisely; it allowed her to reach Delhi by evening. The driver took her straight to an expensive-looking hotel in the Connaught Place area. He was waiting for her at the reception. Bhumi had seen that kind of room only in movies. He had booked the room in advance, and he stayed overnight. It was the second night when they stayed together, and it was as beautiful as the first one. Only this time, they were more comfortable with each other. He was trying his best to make her feel at ease all the time. She had to pinch herself continuously to realise it wasn't a dream.

The next morning, he took her to a private practising lady gynaecologist who confirmed her pregnancy and put her to some tests. She counselled her at length and gave her some medicines that would last a month. They went shopping after that. He was extravagant with shopping as he bought her a complete wardrobe that seemed enough to last the next few years. She tried to protest, but he even got her the dresses keeping in mind her body shape spanning her entire pregnancy.

That night brought further surprises as he disclosed his

future plans. He was going to apply for her passport and would use his resources to get it on an urgent basis. He told her that they were leaving for a foreign posting in ten days. He was considerate enough to ask for her opinion. On her part, she was ready to live anywhere as long as she was with him.

Bhumi's father found her letter in the pocket of his trousers that hung behind the door. She had poured her heart out on it and it was apparent that she had suffered a lot at the hands of her stepmother, though she had never complained much. Apart from anger, he also felt guilty and ashamed for not being able to protect his beloved daughter as much as he should have. But his wife had different plans. She left no stone unturned in her efforts to defame Bhumi. She opined that she had brought great shame to the family.

"The whole society is laughing behind our back; nobody would marry their kids to ours now. It's your fault entirely; you were always the one to defend her. Now see the result."

She would often say such things to him, using the incidence to score further upon her already shaken husband. Losing his hold in family matters, he silently prayed for the wellbeing of his daughter.

Twenty days after reaching New Delhi, Bhumi embarked on her maiden flight and her first journey outside the country. It was the beginning of a new life. Coming from a small town and a laid back and routine life, it was as drastic a change as it could be. She was awestruck and did not know how to react and struggled to keep pace with life on a fast lane. But she had Veer by her side, he was solid as always- comforting her and boosting her confidence all the time.

Whenever he would sense that she was feeling sad for what she had left behind, he would promise her that everything was going to be fine with time. She believed him and felt excited about life with him. In fact, she felt excited about a lot of things. One of those was living on foreign land.

They landed at 'Aeroport de la Pointe Larue' or simply Seychelles International Airport which is located on the island of Mahe near the capital city of Victoria. The country was Seychelles, an archipelago of about one hundred and fifteen small islands in the Indian Ocean, situated about fifteen hundred kilometres east of mainland East Africa. The island of Mahe' is home to its capital Victoria. Together, it's called 'Victoria Mahe".

Way back in the 17th and 18th centuries, it served as a transit point for trade between Asia and Africa. After the French, it was the British who assumed full control of Seychelles after the surrender of Mauritius, its neighbour, in 1814. It gained independence from the British in 1976 when James Mancham became its first President. But the very next year, in 1977, a 'coup d'e'tat' by France Albert Rene ousted him. In fact, Seychelles has a history of coup attempts, there were several against President Rene over the years and India had been in the thick of things on more occasions than one.

In 'coup d'e'tat attempt of 1981 by Mike Hoare, an Air India plane was high jacked by the mercenaries to escape successfully. Again in 1986, during an attempted coup led by Seychelles defence minister Ogilvy Berlouis, President Rene requested help from India, who on its part, sent its naval vessel 'INS Vidhyagiri' to port Victoria and thwarted the attempt.

Keeping in mind the strategic location of Seychelles in the Indian Ocean and its history of political coups, Lt. Col. Veer Pratap Singh was appointed as the cultural attaché at the Indian embassy in Victoria Mahe'. But it was an alibi, he was mainly appointed by the Research and Analysis Wing with the sole duty of ensuring that the former French colony remains more or less democratically peaceful and cooperative towards Indian cause.

Before coming over to Seychelles in the capacity of the 'partner' of India's cultural attaché, the last thing Bhumi did was to post a letter through Veer to Sunita. She owed her an explanation.

To say that her life changed in foreign shores would be an understatement. She had always been an introvert, fond of living in her own dream world. Now with a lot of attention towards her, she felt like a rabbit in glaring sunlight. It was a solace that the island country was scarcely populated and was breathtakingly beautiful. The weather was moderate, and there were hills all around. Although they were not as high as those back home, they were covered with green forests and provided familiar environs. With the Indian Ocean on the other side, she found the place peacefully beautiful.

For Veer, this was nothing new. It was a duty that he looked forward to fulfilling with the best of his capabilities. He also had an additional duty of training Bhumi about what was expected from the better half of an important embassy official. He would take her to all those official functions and parties, where the protocol demanded and would always introduce her as his 'partner.' It was a rather safe word, and she was aware of the constraints that he had to adhere to. Sometimes, she felt he wanted to tell her something, but then he would refrain from it. The divorce case with his wife was in its final stages. Till then the status quo was to be maintained, he had told her.

They had moved into a beautiful double storied bungalow close to the High Commission of India at Le

Chantier in Victoria. It was a French-styled building, bright yellow in colour, and it possessed a lovely lawn upfront. Veer had set up his study on the ground floor, and they had their bedroom overlooking the garden on the first floor.

When Veer would go to his office, she used to make herself busy in household work and gardening, her favourite activity. Within fifteen days, their garden began to show remarkable improvements. She added many new things to it, got new pots and plants, and rearranged them to her likings. But however hard she might try, after years of hard domestic labor meted out at the hands of her stepmother, the work didn't feel like doing much. It wasn't enough work to keep her busy, and her mind would wander a lot, often going back to father and Sunita. There was guilt buried somewhere deep within, that would refuse to go no matter how hard she might try with the distractions.

But all this would change as soon as Veer was back in the evening. They would have their evening tea together in the garden where she would show him her new collection of plants. He was always enthusiastic and showed great interest and was fast learning the names of new plants and trees. Despite being a student of Humanities, Bhumi seemed to know a lot about flora and fauna. It was evident that she was sensitive towards all living beings, be that plants or animals.

One day, the morning sickness grappled her. The signs of pregnancy were beginning to show. He knew that she needed to see a doctor and a good one at that. When she was back from the washroom, he took her into his arms and said, "Maybe we shall go and see a doctor. Do you have any medicines left?"

"No. They are almost finished. The doctor in Delhi had

asked to come at the end of the month," She replied.

"We are way past that time. I will arrange for one today and let you know."

Using his forefinger and left thumb, he pushed her chin up and looking into her eyes, asked,

"How are you feeling now?"

"I am better. For the past few days, I just feel like this in the morning. But it always gets better after some time,"

She replied innocently and then asked,

"Is it necessary to see the doctor?"

"This morning sickness is the symptom of pregnancy. I have..."

He stopped and then asked, "You look worried. Why?"

"I...I hate injections. I am scared of the needles."

She looked terrified. He smiled, "Don't worry; I will try to find a doctor who doesn't believe in needles then."

He patted her reassuringly as he left for work.

Veer came home early that day; they were to go and see a doctor. He told her he had found a good one who was also an important citizen of that small island country. He was trained in England and incidentally, was the only son of the President of the country. He headed the department of gynecology at the government hospital in Victoria.

Located at the northern end of the island of Mahe, the Seychelles hospital is the 'District General Hospital' that provides specialist inpatient and outpatient medical facilities to the citizens. It is a double storied building with red slanting roofs and carved wrought iron railings fitted on corridors of the first floor. It is surrounded by serene lush green hilly vegetation.

If Bhumi wasn't surprised to see such a young doctor in the first place, then she certainly was when he spoke for the first time. The doctor seemed to be in his late twenties and was fair enough to pass as a westerner. Bhumi was already confused about her pregnancy, and on top of that, now being examined by an extremely handsome young male doctor put her in a fix. Unable to make a move, she anxiously looked towards her partner. He nodded reassuringly. Sensing her confusion and guessing her nationality correctly, the doctor suddenly spoke,

"*Aap pareshan na ho*, everything will be alright."

It did give Bhumi enough confidence to stand up and move behind the curtains for examination. The doctor was a gentle soul and possessed that uncanny ability to put his patients at ease.

At the end of it, she softly asked the doctor,

"How come you know Hindi so well?"

He smiled,

"Oh! Actually, my great grandfather came from India. They were the traders of Indian spices. My parents have ensured that I keep links to my roots alive."

"Oh!" was all she could say.

The doctor prescribed some medicines. Everything was normal, he assured her. She had to come again in a week for some tests.

On their way back, Veer said to her,

"I think we have got a good doctor."

She nodded silently.

CHAPTER 7

A Hidden Truth And A Great Loss

Next week, Veer wasn't able to accompany her to the hospital. The President of India was scheduled to visit the island country later in the month, and he had to attend meetings to oversee the security arrangements.

"Good morning Mrs. Singh. Good to see you again."

The doctor greeted her with a smile as soon as he saw her. As he never bothered to look at the papers, it was apparent that he remembered her name from the last meeting.

She smiled in return.

"By the way, I forgot to tell you last time. My name is..."

"Dr. James, I know. It's there outside your cabin."

She said hurriedly as she completed his sentence.

"But it's only half a name. You will be happy to know my complete name. My name is James Shriram. Yet another thing that I have inherited from my Indian forefathers."

He was grinning.

Bhumi began to feel really good. It was comforting to have a smiling doctor, especially if he possessed an Indian surname in some foreign country. But that feel-good factor proved to be extremely short-lived and it evaporated as soon as an attendant initiated the process of extracting the blood samples from her forearms in the pathology lab. She was so panicked that eventually, Dr. James had to be called to pacify her. He ended up holding her hands as the needle was put into her shivering forearms.

After that horrifying experience, he invited her to his chambers for a cup of reconciliatory coffee.

"You need not call my surname 'Shriram' every time you call upon me, Mrs. Singh. People back in India say enough of it, I believe."

He grinned as he took a sip from his coffee.

"Dr. James or simply James would be better."

Even Bhumi felt better as she left for home.

Next week, during an official party at the British High Commission in a Mahe, Bhumi was surprised as she heard someone call her name from behind. She was sitting quietly by herself in a corner.

"Good evening Mrs. Singh. I trust you are feeling good tonight."

She recognized the voice and found Dr. James standing with Veer as she looked in that direction. He looked different, even handsomely boyish as he smiled.

"As Col. told me that you were here, I just wanted to say hello," He was saying.

"And also that you need not worry about the needles anymore. We will find some other ways."

Bhumi blushed as she recalled her over the board reaction at the lab. As she prepared to say something, someone called Dr. James. As he excused himself, he grabbed Veer's hand

and took him along to meet the caller. She watched them leave. He seemed to be an easygoing person, she thought.

The impending tour of the President of India made Veer a very busy person. The world dynamics had changed a lot, especially after American interference in Iraq. Terrorism was beginning to pose threats internationally. Anything could happen even in an unassumingly small country like Seychelles. The protocol called for elaborate arrangements, and Lt. Col. Veer was the head of security. He called upon Dr. James, his new friend, to take good care of Bhumi when he was not around. He arranged for her weekly visits to the hospital.

But it was in the market where she got a chance to see the other side of her gynecologist. She had gone to 'Peoples Supermarket' located on Mont Fleuri as they used to stack some frozen Indian foods as well when she saw him with a shopping basket in hand. Even he was buying the Indian stuff. As she decided upon whether to disturb him or not, he instinctively looked in her direction.

"Nice to see you exploring the local markets, Mrs. Singh."

He smiled as he began to walk towards her.

"And nice to find you buying Indian groceries, Dr. James."

She smiled back, peeping into his basket.

"Mother's insistence. I love preparing dishes for her, and Indian curry is her all-time favourite."

The mention of the family instantly made her sad. He saw it on her face.

"I can assume you are fine, especially after seeing you

here in the supermarket."

"Ya, I am o.k."

She felt silent.

"Maybe I will cook you dinner someday as well. But for now, allow me to drop you home. Are you done with shopping?"

"Ya, not many things are available here. No... I have got my vehicle to take me ba..."

"There are other places around where you can find Indian stuff. And I have promised the Col. to look after you. It would be a crime not to drop you home."

She was cut short in her speech.

It was difficult to argue with the doctor. On the way back, he asked her a lot about life back home. He wanted to know everything about India and seemed quite excited. She felt sad that she couldn't disclose much.

She was now into the third month of her pregnancy. For the past few days, Veer would come quite late in the night. She would try to remain awake, waiting for him. But he insisted that she shouldn't stay awake for that long, it wasn't good for her and the baby. He always had to get up early and leave for office. Then he won't be home even for lunch. There wasn't much for her to do either. It was a new thing for Bhumi. Back home, her mother wouldn't allow her to be idle even for a single minute. Now the thoughts of father and Sunita came flooding. She tried to keep herself busy with the gardening, but there was a limit to it.

One week passed like that. One day, in the afternoon, she felt so bored that she decided to relive the past. She looked for the letters that she had written as a teenager to Veer, the poet. Maybe they were in his study. She came down the hallway to search for them. Veer was meticulous with his stuff, she knew that. His study was well organised, he had a place for everything. She began by looking into his drawers. She remembered the file from the day of the storm. It was nowhere to be seen. She searched and searched, he definitely carried it when he left India. There were piles of books on the shelves, but no file was in sight. Maybe it was in the cabinet. She tried to open it but found it locked. She looked around and saw the drawer. She opened the drawer, but there wasn't any file in it. What it did contain was a bunch of keys. Probably they were the keys to the cabinet.

She sat down and tried one of the keys. The cabinet opened on the second try. There was a pile of files inside it. She picked up the topmost one. It read 'Official correspondences.' Then there were some other official files. She searched in another pile; it was marked 'personal.'

The first file read 'Publishers.' It contained letters from his publishers. She kept looking for the one marked as 'Fan' as she went down the pile. Then she came across the one that was marked as 'wife.' For a moment, she thought it was meant for her. But as she opened it, she realised it belonged to his first wife.

Bhumi had seen only a few photographs of his wife and that encompassed her entire knowledge about the lady. Veer had told her about their ongoing divorce case. The next file seemed to contain legal proceedings of the same, for it was marked 'Divorce-Legal.' Suddenly, she got curious; she wanted it to get over as soon as possible. She opened the file and began reading through the pages. There were notices and counter-notices from parties, allegations and counter-allegations, arguments and counter-arguments. There was a legal notice from his wife's lawyer, claiming the compensation for her and …

"What is that? Am I reading, right?"

Bhumi murmured as she read further. Her heart sank as she couldn't believe her eyes. Frantically, she re-read the notice again. Then she read the next few pages. Everything was as clear as was the sunshine outside. Inside the study of Lt. Col. Veer, Bhumi's mind went into complete darkness. Among other things, Veer and his wife were also fighting for the custody of their… only daughter.

It was unfathomable. He had never ever mentioned his daughter. She sank onto the floor. As she read further, she found that Veer had applied to the judicial courts for permission to meet his daughter as often as he would like to and the Judge had directed his wife to allow him to meet her twice a month. In another undertaking, he had claimed that being a chronic alcoholic, his wife wasn't fit to look after an eight-year-old girl. Even the girl was eight now.

She got up from the floor. Reading those letters wasn't in her mind anymore. She felt a certain heaviness in her legs as she slowly climbed the stairs. Once inside her bedroom, she collapsed on to the bed. Tears began to roll down her eyes. How could he fail to tell her the truth, especially when he was going to be a father once again? It wasn't about his daughter as it was about hiding the truth. She had never felt that kind of betrayal in her life, she thought as she cried profusely.

Veer came home early than usual that evening. He found Bhumi sitting on the bed; she hadn't left that place since afternoon. He felt she wasn't keeping well. He immediately came to her side. Sitting on the edge of the bed, he tried holding her hand as he inquired, "Are you alright, Bhumi? You look unwell."

She drew her hands away from his. He instinctively knew something was wrong. He looked into her eyes.

"What happened? Is anything wrong?"

She just looked the other way in response. He waited for a while; she kept on looking down on the floor.

"How would I know if something is bothering you if you do not tell me Bhumi?"

He tried again.

After what appeared to be a very long pause, as he lifted her chin with his fingers, he saw that her eyes were filled with tears.

"Now, would you tell me the reason, please?"

He tried to wipe away the tears; she removed his hands from her face. He was a poet, he could sense the pain.

"You have a daughter, don't you?"

She spluttered as she sobbed. Veer's face turned pale, his gaze immediately fell. He couldn't say anything.

"Why didn't you tell me, Veer? I left everything for you, and you had no faith in me all the time."

He remained silent.

"I believed you. I even left my father just to be with you. And you..."

"I always wanted to tell you, Bhumi, but every time I tried, I... stopped."

"Stopped for what? You never believed me, that's what stopped you, *na?*"

Her voice was rising.

"No, I stopped because I was scared."

"Please don't give me this rubbish. Lt. Col. Veer Pratap Singh is a scared man. No, I can't believe you anymore."

She said as she stood up to leave.

"No, Bhumi, please listen. Believe me, I always wanted to tell you, I would have told you any day."

He stood up with her and tried to stop her from leaving.

"No, Veer, you had enough chances to tell me these days. Given a chance, you would have hidden everything from me forever."

Her voice was full of agony as she tried to repulse his efforts. She began to move away from him and out of the room. He followed her, pleading.

"I know you are feeling hurt, but please..."

He was trying to hold her by the elbow.

"Please leave me alone…"

As she tried to move away from him, Bhumi didn't realise that she was on the edge of the stairs that were going down the hallway. She lost her balance and fell steeply. He tried to move forward to stop her from falling, but he was too late. She came down the flight of stairs and landed on the hallway with a loud thud. Veer rushed behind her.

"Bhumi… Bhumi…"

He cried agonisingly as he put her head on his lap. There wasn't a response in Bhumi.

Dr. James Shriram was about to call it a day and leave for home when the ambulance came rushing into the hospital. He was the one who personally attended the patient who was still unconscious.

It was only the next morning when Bhumi regained her consciousness. Veer was sitting by her bedside, he hadn't left the place since last night, and he looked distraught. He tried a faint smile as he saw her struggling to open her eyes. There was a nurse in the room, as well. Seeing the patient coming to senses, she said, "I would call the doctor."

As she left the room, Veer came forward and patted on her head. Bhumi couldn't fathom the chain of events at once. All she could feel was severe pain in her head; she looked around the room as she tried to remember everything.

Just as Veer was about to say something, Dr. James entered the room.

"Welcome back, Mrs. Singh. How do you feel now?"

He said cheerfully as he checked her eyes.

"Where I am Doctor?"

Her voice was fragile and her face was filled with pain.

"Good, you remember me, ma'am. You had a bad accident at home last evening as you fell off the stairs. Do you remember that?"

The doctor asked as he kept his check-up going.

"Last ...evening?"

She was struggling to remember the sequence of events.

"Ya, Veer brought you here unconscious. And he hasn't left your side ever since."

He said as he patted Veer on his back.

Bhumi looked in his direction. Suddenly she remembered everything. She looked away.

"Maybe you should take some rest now. She is going to be alright," The doctor said to Veer.

"But…"

"Please do not worry. We wouldn't like to have you as a patient now. Even she needs to rest as she will have to be here for a few more days. You can wait in my chamber; I will just join you for a cup of coffee after finishing my checkup."

Dr. James insisted, ignoring Veer's plea.

Back in the chamber, after fifteen minutes, Dr. James joined Veer over coffee.

"How is she, James."

Veer inquired in a concerned voice.

"She will be alright. We will keep her under observation for a few days. But it's more about mental trauma than physical pain now, I suspect."

The doctor replied.

"Means?"

"She is already shaken. And when she would hear about her loss, I mean, it would be challenging for her to cope mentally."

"Yeah, I understand. That is what I fear now," Veer replied in a dejected voice.

He looked gravely concerned.

"But we have to tell her nevertheless, maybe in the evening today. Then we will try to manage accordingly."

"I would be grateful if you break the news to her. Maybe, it will be easier for her to cope if she hears it from you, James."

"I will try. Let's do it in the evening then."

Dr. James assured him as he got up from the chair.

"You have been one lucky girl, Mrs. Singh."

Dr. James said enthusiastically as Veer entered the hospital room. He briefly had to go to his office during the day. Bhumi looked in his direction for a while and then turned her eyes back towards the doctor again.

"Only you can see something good out of it, doctor," She replied sadly.

Dr. James refused to lose his confidence.

"I am speaking on medical terms, Mrs. Singh. It could have been a lot worse."

"That it already is."

She did not look even once towards Veer, who was listening sincerely to the conversation. He was robbed of any chance to explain himself since she fell off the stairs and went unconscious. The talks were moving towards the most difficult phase. He nervously shifted on his legs.

"No, because of mishap…"

Dr. James tried to come to the point of revelation, "I mean… the miscarriage that has happened because of the fall…"

She looked towards him at once. Her eyes went wide, and her lips parted in astonishment.

"What…. Do you…"

She couldn't say much.

"We weren't able to do anything about that Mrs. Singh. The baby was already lost by the time you were brought here."

Tears began to roll down Bhumi's eyes; she made no attempt to hide them. Her beautiful face was filled with so much pain and agony that both the men couldn't say anything for a while. She slipped down on to her bed and cried uncontrollably. Veer came forward to console her and tried to put his hands on her head.

She buried her face in the pillow and between her sobs, murmured, "Please leave me alone. It's all because of you that I have lost my baby. I do not want to live anymore."

Dr. James tried to pacify her.

"It indeed is a great loss. But there's so much more to life. We are glad that you are alive, Mrs. Singh."

"I am pained that I did not die."

She cried.

CHAPTER 8

The Alienation

Bhumi was kept in the hospital for three more days. During the time, she regained some of her health physically but mentally, she didn't get better. She cried much and spoke little. For Veer, he was caught between home and office; there was so much work to do at both the fronts. While he was exhausted intellectually at his office, he was emotionally spent at the hospital. Bhumi refused to forgive him. If his hiding of personal secrets from her wasn't enough, the loss of her baby was such a shock that she wasn't even prepared to listen to his explanations. It was like a double blow. She behaved indifferently towards him, and that was what pained him the most.

Even when she was shifted back home, things did not improve. Deep within, she held him responsible for the loss of her baby. She had taken all the risks just to have her baby and be with him, and now she felt like everything was lost. She missed her hometown very much, she would often think about her father and Sunita, her own people she had left behind, to be with the man who had proved himself to be unfaithful. Now she had no one to share her agony with, she did not feel like talking to Veer, however hard he may try. There was a communication gap between them at home, and they spoke bare minimum.

One week after her return from the hospital, Veer called upon Dr. James at the hospital. Even he was devoid of someone he could share his agonies with.

"She holds me responsible for everything, James, and she is almost right. But I am the slave of my own circumstances. I can no longer watch her like this, I need your help."

He opened up; it was really rare coming from him. Even Dr. James felt sorry; he kind of liked the family, especially Bhumi. He himself was a man of simplicity and she was one such girl. She needed help and it was difficult to deny that.

"Ok. I would come and see her in the evening. Let's see what can be done."

He assured Veer.

Bhumi was sitting in the garden that bore a deserted look. She had no inclination towards looking after the plants that were once so dear to her. The coming of Dr. James was like a breath of fresh air in what generally seemed like a gloomy evening. He wondered how much the mental state of its inhabitants could do to the overall atmosphere of a home. Veer was yet to arrive. Stopping his car in the porch, he went straight to her and greeted cheerfully,

"Great to see you spending your evenings amid nature Mrs. Singh."

Bhumi looked in his direction; she managed a faint smile of acknowledgment.

"How do you feel now? I trust you're better."

He inquired, taking a chair in front of her. She nodded and kept looking down. He waited patiently. When she refused to break the silence, he probed further.

"I have heard that Indians, especially those from the northern mountains are great hosts."

He was smiling. She looked up and feeling embarrassed, said, "I am sorry doctor. I should have asked. What would you like to have?"

"Just a cup of coffee but only if you would have it too."

"Okay."

She smiled for the first time and called for help.

"Your garden is beautiful, Mrs. Singh."

"It once was," She replied.

"Can I ask you something?" He asked.

She raised her eyes in askance and waited.

"I understand that these have been very trying times for you. And I know how it feels when you lose someone who was a part of you."

He turned serious. Bhumi couldn't fathom what the doctor was saying. She looked towards him and questioned, "Do you really, doctor?"

"Yeah, I too have been through some tough times."

He looked up in the horizon.

"You don't know anything about my life doctor."

"Sure, I do not know. But then even you don't about mine either."

"There is nothing wrong with yours as compared to mine."

She held her position, wandering in her own gloomy world.

"I lost my only sister, my best friend, on this very day last year."

She was taken aback. He continued looking nowhere. Dr. James seemed lost in his own world.

"I…I am so very sorry. I had no idea."

She said apologetically. For once, she forgot about her own pain. The doctor looked in her direction and smiled, "It's ok. The one thing I have learned is that life is too unpredictable, yet too beautiful. You do no good to the dead by being sad."

"How…how did it happen, if I may ask?"

"Oh, it was …she was killed when someone broke into her house in London where she studied. She had called me in the evening and seemed so happy."

He smiled sadly.

"It's so unfortunate. It must have been so hard for you and family."

Bhumi was genuinely sympathetic, her thoughts went towards him.

"Actually she was just my age, only a year older, but much smarter than me. A brilliant student and so full of life. But more than anything else, she was my friend, philosopher and guide, she was everything."

It seemed he was on the verge of crying, Dr. James Shriram, head of gynaecology at Seychelles' premier hospital and the President's only son. For a moment, she felt her personal grief wasn't that great after all.

He regained composure quickly and said smilingly, "We all think we have been mistreated by God, we did not deserve it. But there are people far more unfortunate than us out there. When I see them at the hospital, I forget my own pain. That's how I have managed my personal grief and that's why I am here, seeking your help."

"Me? How can I help? I am good for nothing."

Bhumi was surprised.

"That's your perspective at the moment. But from where I see you, you can do wonders, Mrs. Singh."

Dr. James looked genuine in his words. She was still confused.

"I am sorry, but I am unable to understand what you are trying to say, doctor."

She said.

"Actually, in our department of paediatrics at the hospital, we are looking for volunteers who might be able to spend some time with ailing kids. The remuneration might not be great, but this job does give the participant a chance to see life at close quarters and relive one's childhood all over again. I am sure you will prove to be a great volunteer, Mrs. Singh. But of course, only if you agree to be one."

It took a while for Bhumi to realise that she was presented with a proposal. Unable to think, she remained silent. Dr. James waited patiently before adding, "If you can, believe me, ma'am, the kids would love you, and you will love the kids. Life feels a lot better when it's lived for others. I have talked to Veer about this, and even he is quite excited about your new role if you would accept it."

She remained silent.

"Please say yes, ma'am. You can always say no anytime if you do not like this responsibility. I am just asking you to give it a try."

He kind of pleaded. She opened her lips after a long pause, "On one condition, only."

"And that is…"

He was excited and puzzled at the same time.

"That you won't call me ma'am or Mrs. Singh anymore. My name is Bhumi and I believe you should call me that only."

She smiled genuinely for the first time in several days.

"Done."

Dr. James grinned like a teenage boy.

On her very first day at the hospital, Bhumi was welcomed warmly. Dr. James enthusiastically showed her around the hospital. To begin with, it brought the old memories back, and she regretted her decision of being a volunteer at a place, she had only bad memories of. But on the other hand, she felt relieved as well. She was getting mad sitting idle at home surrounded by all kinds of negative thoughts. Thankfully, the department of paediatrics was at the other end of the building, and it opened into a beautiful garden at the back. It also had a children park and mountains were visible from there. There were kids of all ages and colours, they mostly came from various islands scattered around, that together made up the country. The hospital contained the best facilities inside Seychelles. Bhumi had only seen the government hospital at Mussoorie, and this hospital was far more clean and far less crowded than that.

The kids suffered from different kinds of ailments. She was surprised to know about the disease called AIDS and how it affected kids as small as six months of age. Cancer was another dreaded disease as was tuberculosis among the poor suffering from malnutrition. The department was short on trained hands; she was explained about her duties and what was expected of her as a volunteer. Her duty was to begin at eight in the morning and would only be over after the complimentary lunch that she could have at the hospital cafeteria. Dr. James had arranged an official car for her as well.

By the end of the first day, she did not have enough chance to mingle with kids as most of the time was spent on explanations and formalities. As she reached home, old memories came flooded in, as if some dam was broken. But she was too tired to think about anything.

Before succumbing to sleep, she still wasn't sure if she had made the right decision about the hospital thing.

Veer was intently watching the progress made by Bhumi. She would get up early in the morning and be ready before her transport would arrive. She would also ensure that all the preparations for his breakfast were in place before she would leave. In spite of her bitter experiences of late, she was spot on when it came to performing her duties. By the end of the first week, he felt her behaviour towards him wasn't that cold.

At the hospital, Bhumi began to develop a liking towards her new job as well. More often than not, she would share her lunch with Dr. James at the cafeteria or instead Dr. James would share his lunch with her as his mother would often pack one for him. While the doctor shared his meal, she would share her stories of kids with him. He watched her happily as she would explain everything with excitement, her face turning into a kaleidoscope of emotions. As long as she was at the hospital, she began to forget about her personal grief. Ironically, it really was at home that she felt alone. Although she had begun to interact with Veer when it was absolutely necessary, she hadn't forgiven him entirely.

Veer understood that she needed time for her wounds to heal. He was patient and apologetic.

For Bhumi, Dr. James was a different character. He was selfless professionally and full of life personally. She was inspired a lot by his approach towards life. Sometimes, he would drop her back and share a cup of coffee in her garden. He would also intimate Veer on how she was working so hard to bringing her life back on track. Veer trusted him with the task. He was one such man.

In a few months, the ailing kids of the District General Hospital of Victoria Mahe became an integral part of Bhumi's life. And given her popularity among them, it could be said that she became an essential part of them as well. She also became a known face at the President's Palace as James had taken her to meet his parents on a few occasions where he introduced her as an 'Angel from India.'

Even Veer had begun to feel that things were about to turn normal again when events took a sudden and unexpected turn.

It was a normal day at the office when he received the orders. It clearly stated that he was to report back to Delhi headquarters without any delay. Although intelligence bodies always worked that way, Veer was still taken by surprise. Despite his contacts in New Delhi, he had failed to see it coming. What was more, it wasn't the routine 'calling back the envoy for consultations' kind of step. What Veer did come to know was, the request had come to his parent body- the RAW, through the Ministry of External Affairs in New Delhi.

Whatever may be the reason, it confirmed that Veer's days in Seychelles were cut short with immediate effect and he was not supposed to return back. He will have to make arrangements fast, he thought. Bhumi would be at the hospital. What will she think about the new developments? Will she be happy? Will she be sad? Then how will he manage to keep her with him in India? After all, there was still some time to go before the divorce. It was quite easy to live together in this secluded part of the world without raising a doubt. But this anonymity wasn't possible in India. He first needed to talk to her and inform her about this new development before anything else.

Bhumi was teaching the kids in the park when he reached the hospital. Veer watched her from a distance. She looked absolutely happy in the company of small children. He waited for some time as he contemplated the timing of breaking the news to her. It felt criminal to spoil the happiness that he witnessed in her in a long long time. Dr. James was not in his chambers. He decided to delay it till the afternoon; the hospital was hardly a place for such matters.

Bhumi was surprised to find him home at that hour; he generally used to come late. She was even more amazed when he called her to his study.

"I have something important to discuss with you Bhumi."

He was saying in his deep husky voice. It didn't have the same effect on her these days. She kept standing and stared towards him.

"If you would sit down for a while, please."

He requested. She took a chair opposite him.

"I have been called back to New Delhi. We have to leave."

She was so surprised that she couldn't say anything. Apart from her facial expressions, nothing changed, she sat there motionlessly. He waited for the news to sink in.

"When?" She finally managed to murmur.

"The day after."

"The day after tomorrow? What do you mean?"

"I have my orders, Bhumi. I cannot do anything about that. We have to leave, so it's better we must begin preparing fast."

"How could it be possible so quickly? There's so much to do. What will I say to James, and what will happen to the kids at the hospital? Do you have any idea?"

Her beautiful face was immediately filled with pain. It was hard for him, as well. 'I always want to give you all the pleasures, and yet I end up giving only the pains,' he wanted to say. Yet, he ended up saying, "I will talk to James about it. You will find another hospital if you wish."

And then he added, "In India."

"Do you have any emotions, Veer? You know, I always used to ask you how an army man could write such beautiful lines, have such a soft heart. Maybe you didn't have any, it was all lies."

"Be rationale Bhumi. I am a government servant, posted here on international duty. We have to follow orders."

"It's you who might be a government servant, not me, Veer. And I don't know about the government, but I have to follow your orders for sure, *na.*"

"It's not like that, Bhumi. I have always been pressed by circumstances."

"Yes, you have always been pressed by circumstances to hide the truth."

It was apparent that she still felt the pain. He became silent for a while.

"There's no use wasting our time like this because we don't have much of it. Let's start preparing to leave; I have a lot to do."

He stood up to leave.

"What about the three months contract that I have signed with the hospital, then?"

She shouted on his back. He stopped and said,

"I will find you another one. You can have my word on that."

"No. This time, I will keep my words for a change."

She left him standing there, perplexed by her sudden outbursts.

Veer came back to his chair and sat there, motionless. It was proving more complicated than he had anticipated. His intuition was telling him that everything wasn't right. He thought about the difficulties that waited for him in India. On top of it, there were the arrangements that he had to make at his domestic front. He had an eight years old daughter to look after; he had the most difficult wife to get rid of. And now, he had this task of hiding the love of his life from his own people. He closed his eyes and tried hard to think of solutions.

It was early the next morning when Veer met Dr. James at the hospital. He had just started his day.

"I need some urgent help, James."

He said as he came in, without wasting any precious time.

"I know. You have to leave Col."

Dr. James smiled sadly and then added, "Our beautiful country. Time to say goodbye."

"Bound by duty, we are the slaves of circumstances."

"True. As it's said in Bhagwad Gita."

"But I have some other problems at hand, James."

"I am aware of that too. It's regarding Bhumi?" James questioned.

"Yes. She doesn't want to leave. She wants to be with kids and complete her assignment at this hospital."

"Ya, she was here first thing in the morning, Col. "

"Would you please make her see the reason, James? I mean..."

"I have already tried to...argue with her. But it seems it's the first time in her life when she has got a reason to... live for a cause. She is kind of feeling worthy of her own life being with the kids. You must see her while she is here."

"That I appreciate as well. She is doing great in that sense, and it wasn't possible without you, James."

"But I can't leave her over here."

Dr James waited for a while before replying,

"It's a three-month contract, Colonel and one month have already passed. Knowing her mental status, I would suggest she must be given a chance to live her life her own way. It will be over in a few months then she will join you in India."

"But she hasn't ever been alone. There are so many issues to look at, so many loose ends…"

"Everything happens the first time, when it happens for the first time, Colonel," James smiled,

"You need not worry about them. They can be taken care of. There won't be an issue with the visa as it's a government contract. It isn't a big deal, Col. It can be managed."

Veer couldn't say anything for a long time. James waited patiently.

"Let me give it a thought, James."

He stood up to leave. He was unsure about so many things. What he was sure about was that James was the second most powerful man in that country, and he was the kind of man who could be trusted.

CHAPTER 9

As Fate Would Have It

One day after meeting Dr. James at the hospital, Col. Veer Pratap Singh took a solo flight back home. With the airplane, his thoughts took a flight as well. The last forty-eight hours had been like a mental rollercoaster ride of emotions. Personally, it had proved to be very difficult for both of them, especially towards the end. It was the last thing that they had prepared for. Bhumi's eyes were moist as he had said goodbye, she fought hard to contain her emotions. As he had turned back one final time, he had seen James patting her back while she looked the other way. At least, James was there, he had been the saving grace. He was really influential and had arranged for her stay at the palace itself. She was in safe hands for sure, and he had promised him to send her back in a few months. Veer believed him, there was nothing much that he could do either, he thought. He changed his position and tried to shift his focus into the future.

Now at least he would have the time and freedom to make proper arrangements, too many wrong actions have taken place because of the lack of them, he thought. In hindsight, maybe it was good that Bhumi decided to stay back for a while. It was difficult to contain an intellectually strong girl like her without a worthwhile engagement for long. He won't make further mistakes with her, he promised himself.

A lot was waiting to be done in India as well. Personally, he had to get his life back on track, especially regarding the three ladies in her life. And professionally? Veer looked out of the window. The airplane had climbed over the clouds and was gliding smoothly. He felt a sudden turbulence building inside his head.

What if the rumours he had heard about New Delhi were true?

He closed his eyes to get that temporary respite.

The official residence of the President of Seychelles is known as 'State House.' It's an old building, but it is exceptionally well kept. Built for the Governor-General when it was still a British colony in 1910, it's an aesthetically looking structure, a two-storied colonial architecture with white pillars upfront. The building was renovated in 1976, immediately after Seychelles became independent.

The State House has a vast expanse of green lawns upfront. Bhumi got her room on the first floor, and whenever she stepped out in the portico, she would see the same greenery. James too had his bedroom on the same floor; it was at the far end. But he would check up on her as often as he could, to make her feel comfortable and welcomed.

Bhumi immersed herself in work at the hospital. More often than not, James would have to drag her home. Her appetite was also gone since Veer left for India. She would eat a bare minimum.

'It's impossible to survive on such scarce energy.' James often warned her at the dining table, though in a lighter tone. But there seemed no respite from the emotional turmoil that she was going through.

One fine evening, Dr. James stormed into her workplace.

"I cannot bear this anymore."

He complained in such a childish way that even Bhumi was forced to smile.

"What is that you cannot bear doctor?"

She enquired amid her smile.

"The hiding of some secrets from you."

Her jaws fell immediately; she turned dead serious, even sad. She was like a scared rabbit. She didn't say anything in return, just looked at him enquiringly.

"That the best Indian restaurant in the country is just a few kilometres from here."

He said hurriedly, realising that she wasn't in a mental state to play along for long.

She seemed disappointed. James came forward and touched her elbow.

"Come on, Bhumi. We will have to go home to change. I cannot go out without my evening shower, you know."

She remained reluctant.

"I can't go."

"But why not?"

He demanded.

"Because I don't feel like it. And the food at home is good."

"Ya. That I know, being a daily witness to how much you relish the food."

He was smiling. She remained quiet.

"Bhumi, it's not only about the food. You need a break too. I have promised the Col. that I will take good care of you."

He immediately sensed that he had made a mistake

by mentioning Veer, for she turned even more sombre. He tried to distract her.

"What's more, I have also found out they have a chef who belongs to North Indian Mountains. Who knows he might know you as well."

She suddenly was frightened, old memories came flooding.

"No, I won't go. Please don't force me."

She almost pleaded. James was surprised by the sudden change in her behaviour. She even looked disturbed.

"It's alright, we won't go," He said hurriedly.

"But can we go for a walk on the beach on our way back? I won't take a no this time."

He said adamantly. She smiled,

"Let's go then."

She looked normal again. James was more intrigued than before, it was difficult for him to understand this strange but lovely mountain girl.

But he was not the only person who was intrigued. People at Research and Analysis Wing in New Delhi were also surprised when Col. Veer Pratap Singh failed to report his comeback at the headquarters following his return from Seychelles.

CHAPTER 10

The Coup And The Vanish

Even Veer was surprised to see his friend Col. Rajesh waiting for him at the arrivals of Indira Gandhi International Airport in New Delhi. It was almost midnight, and there wasn't any explanation for his presence at that odd hour. Once inside his car, Rajesh didn't wait for long.

"There has been some problem Veer."

It was his way of declaring bad news. Veer looked at him questioningly.

"Rumour is, the proceedings for your 'Court Martial' might be initiated."

The tone of Col. Rajesh bore a dejected look. Though Veer tried to keep a straight face, his worst fears were proving to be true.

"And the ground is?"

He asked.

"You're compromising the security of the nation."

Then seeing the traces of confusion on his friend's face, Col. Rajesh added,

"By taking a female companion on a highly sensitive foreign posting and introducing her as your wife, in spite of being married to a different lady."

Col. Veer remained motionless.

"It's your wife's undoing Veer. Apparently, she met someone at a party sometimes during the last month who asked her if she was the original wife of Col. Veer, the cultural attaché at the Indian embassy in Victoria Mahe, then who was the lady with him over there."

"They have collected a lot of pieces of evidence against you in this last month. Now they have converted it into a strong case."

Col. Rajesh was saying.

Veer immediately realised it was a far bigger problem than he had anticipated. It was literally going to be the end of his professional career.

"Where are we heading now?"

Veer suddenly asked.

"To my home, where else?"

Rajesh replied.

"Take me to a hotel instead, Rajesh. I need some time to sort this thing out."

Sensing an absolute resolve in his voice, Col. Rajesh decided to follow his friend's instructions.

Veer opted for an ordinary hotel in the Paharganj area, just opposite the 'New Delhi Railway Station.' His best friend remained with him overnight; it was only in the wee hours the next morning when he returned home with a pile of papers lying in the boot of his car. For him, it was merely a long night. For Veer, it was going to be a very long fight, he suspected.

What he never suspected was that he had seen the last of his best friend.

In fact, no one saw Col. Veer Pratap Singh ever again. Or someone did?

That Bhumi was crazy about water was unknown to James. As soon as they hit the seashore, her mood changed dramatically. She felt so excited that leaving behind James, she immediately ran to meet the incoming waves. James watched intently from a distance. The Sun was setting into the Indian Ocean, and it threw all kinds of colours – from bright orange to yellow and the dark brown, all over the horizon. Below it, the ocean water was shining silvery bright. For James, the girl shone brighter of them all.

He let her play with the waves and sat down to watch. The sea breeze was strong and cool. She gestured towards him to join the waters, he just smiled. When she was all drenched and done, she came and sat beside him.

"It's so beautiful. Thanks for bringing me here," She said.

"I knew you'd like it here. That's why I insisted. But this much?"

James grinned as he threw his hands up in exasperation.

"You know, sometimes I think I know you only to realise it soon that I know nothing about you."

"Am I that difficult a girl?"

She said smilingly.

"That's not what I meant. I mean…"

He hesitated as she raised an eyebrow,

"There's an air of mystery around you. And I like that."

He added the last sentence, hurriedly.

"Life in itself is a mystery doctor. As soon as you think you have got the heck of it, it will toss you upside down."

She was getting poetic after a long time. She liked the mood.

"I didn't know there's a philosopher in you."

"Corrections. It's a poet."

"Really? Yet another hidden facet of your personality."

"It's not a secret to those who know me well."

"I admit that I am yet to know you well. But I am willing, now it's upto you to let me know everything about you."

Looking directly into her eyes, he said it so seriously that Bhumi lowered her gaze and began to look towards the setting Sun.

In New Delhi, India the next day, the Sun was shining brightly in the morning sky when it was officially confirmed that Col. Veer Pratap Singh had mysteriously disappeared from the face of the earth.

"Sir, more than anything else, it seems the case of a young girl falling for a wordsmith that our man has always been."

The boss was informed.

"No traces of any sabotage?" He inquired.

"None so far, sir. We are keeping an eye."

"But why our man fell for the girl. He was a seasoned officer."

"Hard to say, sir. Chances are its human nature. He was dealing with a dysfunctional family for many years, in fact from the very beginning of his married life, without any respite."

"And the discrepancies were first reported by his wife alright?" The boss asked.

"Yes, sir. She bought it to our notice, and although she is suffering from chronic alcoholism, her accusations proved to be correct."

"What a pity. I once served under her father, the late General. A great leader and a thorough gentleman."

He murmured. And then asked, "Any trace of our man?"

"No, sir. Col. Veer Pratap Singh knows the agency inside out. He is one of our very best. It's going to be very difficult to find him unless…"

The boss questioningly raised an eyebrow,

"…he himself decides to show up," The officer completed his sentence.

"You mean, he is hiding on purpose?"

"It seems so, Sir. There's no other explanation."

"Don't give me no for an answer. The agency is not a one-man show. Get your best man out there and let the hunt begin."

The boss thundered and pushed his chair backwards. It was a signal that the meeting was over. The officer stood up to leave. This particular hunt was going to be longer and harder than any other hunt, he suspected.

With its offices near the Reagent's Park in Central London, The Royal College of Obstetricians and Gynaecologists (RCOG) is a professional association working in the field of female pregnancy, childbirth, female sexual and reproductive health. Nearly half of its members are based outside of England. Dr. James Shriram was a member of RCOG. That was why, when he received a letter bearing its emblem consisting of a saintly couple standing on either side of the shield, he took it to be a regular male.

That was the last letter from his pile of official correspondence that he opened at the end of the day. He was about to leave for home, but the letter forced him to stay put for the next half an hour.

Strangely, there were two envelopes inside. One was marked,

To,

Dr. James.

The other was marked

To,

Bhumi.

Both were kept inside the big envelope that looked like the official correspondence from RCOG. He picked up and opened the one that was addressed to him. Expression of grave concern emerged on his handsome face as he read the contents. He read it twice before he picked up the phone and hurriedly began to dial some numbers.

He could have forgotten the other envelope had

Bhumi not entered his chamber as he got up to leave. She immediately sensed that something was wrong.

They missed their daily evening walk by the sea that day as he drove directly to the palace. James seemed thoughtful throughout the drive. On her part, Bhumi chose to keep quiet.

It was 9:30 pm. Bhumi was thinking about the empty dining table at the dinner. It was the first time when she had to eat by herself since she had been there. There was a knock on the door, she responded to find James standing outside. She felt a specific relief as he smiled for the very first time that evening.

"Sorry for my absence at the dinner tonight."

He smiled faintly as he spoke.

"No, it's okay. I am used to be alone these days."

She looked sad.

"There were some pressing problems at work, but you certainly are not one of them. "

He tried to cheer her up.

"Is there anything that I can do?"

She was genuine in her concern.

"No, no…They have been taken care of. You need not worry at all. In fact, I was feeling guilty about missing our evening walk today."

"There isn't a need. The sea is not going anywhere and… neither am I."

She said smilingly. Her beautiful smile distracted his mind for a while. His hand moved to reach for his back pocket that contained the letter addressed to her. He contemplated for a while. Sensing some dilemma, she asked, “If you want to tell me something, you can.”

“Not something that cannot wait for another day.”

His hand failed to reach the pocket.

“You know, you cannot lie with these kinds of eyes.”

She was looking directly into them.

“Nor do I intend to. Let’s go for a walk on the terrace.”

She could feel the tension as he took her hands into his.

The breeze from the sea was cool. She shivered as she stepped out on the terrace. James immediately took out his blazer and put it on her shoulders. She tried to refuse, but he insisted. The lights from the houses on the far hill shone like fireflies against the black backdrop. They reminded her of her hometown, Mussoorie.

“You know, in my hometown, the hills at night are just like that,” She said.

“Do you miss your country, your people?” He asked.

“Ya. I miss them all. More so since Veer left.”

“I know myself and my country are inferior substitutes.”

There was a hint of sadness in his voice. She immediately turned towards him.

“Please do not say that. I did not mean that way. This country is no less home for me now. And you are the finest person that I could have as a …friend.”

She had never been that close, Bhumi was entering into unfamiliar territories. He watched her intently. The fancy light bulbs were illuminating her beautiful face in numerous ways. It felt criminal to take the smile away from such a face. Maybe it was the time to go with the flow. 'Forget about everything and savour the moment ', someone yelled from deep within.

'No. It's not about you; it's about your country, James. You don't have time, and you know that'. Another voice called.

He took a deep breath.

"I have to tell you something, Bhumi…" his voice was shaking as he spoke.

It happened in the wee hours of the night. She had become so worried after what was told by James on the terrace; she prayed all that to be untrue. Bhumi had hardly gone to sleep when she heard loud noises. At first, she thought she was dreaming of bursting firecrackers. But the noises grew louder and louder. As she was getting out of the bed, someone began to knock vigorously at her door. Then she heard her name being called, it was James. She opened the door, and he came in and bolted the door from inside. He looked distraught.

"What is it, James? I heard…"

"It's a military coup against our democratic government that I talked about earlier. We have a history of that. I am thankful to Veer for he informed us in advance. But the conspiracy seems much bigger than we had anticipated, and they have taken us by surprise," He babbled.

"Never mind, we will see to it. But there is hardly any time to waste. Get your passport and other valuables as fast as you can. We have got to go."

"But James…"

"Please Bhumi. There is no time to explain. I will tell you all once things turn normal again. Right now, you are leaving."

He pushed her to work faster. Bhumi could sense the urgency, yet she did not like the idea.

"I don't want to go anywhere."

She pleaded.

"If you have faith in me then trust me. I am only doing

what is best for you."

"And what about you?"

She asked as she collected her belongings and began to put them into a small bag.

"This is my country Bhumi. I cannot leave my parents and my people. They need me."

He took her by the arm and cautiously opened the door. It was all dark outside; someone had put off the lights. Voices of people running here and there filled the atmosphere. It was all chaos. The gunshots continued, they seemed to be coming from across the road. A gun battle was on at the entrance of the palace.

"Hurry up. We gotta run."

James whispered as they ran towards the far end of the long corridor. He took her down through some hidden stairs.

"Here's some cash, you will need it."

James had put a bundle of dollars into her hands as they reached the back of the palace. Bhumi heard a loud, roaring noise. Soon she came to know about the source of that sound. A small helicopter was up and running on what were the plush green back lawns of the Presidential palace during the day. Now it was all dark but for some light emerging from the big flying machine. James withdrew an envelope as they approached the chopper.

"This is the letter from Veer. It is for you; use it to find him when you reach India."

He was shouting to be heard over the loud roar of the machine.

"The chopper will take you to Mauritius. From there,

the Indian embassy will arrange for your safe journey back home. They have been intimated."

He shouted as he helped her climb the chopper. Everything happened so quickly that Bhumi didn't have time to think, her mind was blank.

As she turned to look towards him, their eyes met. She knew she couldn't forget those eyes for the rest of her life. She had seen those kinds of eyes once before.

As the helicopter took off, she looked beyond and found a large group of gun trotting soldiers rushing towards James, who was left standing helplessly on the lawn. As the helicopter went up towards safety, the day was breaking on the far horizon. But deep down, where James stood last, the night was all black.

CHAPTER 11

Return Of The Forbidden Girl

Bhumi had never imagined that her own country would ever feel so alien to her. During the entire flight from Port Luis to New Delhi, she was constantly thinking about James. She prayed and prayed for his survival. He was a great soul, a perfect man who any girl would happily have as her life partner. She even felt guilty about him. She felt helpless.

Now, as she landed at New Delhi international airport, she suddenly realised that she had nowhere to go. It was almost eleven at night when she came out of the arrivals. Devoid of options, she looked for and found a public telephone booth just outside the gates and dialled the solitary phone number given by Veer in the letter that was handed over to her by James in the last moments of her escape. In his usual way, he had written,

"Call this number when you are back in India."

It was the only connection left between them. Even in distress, James possessed the mind to remind her of the same. Oh, James! It was hard to get him out of her mind. There was no way she could repay him in this lifetime. Now she had a problem at hand and even he was not there to help her out this time.

But she had another thing to look forward to. Soon she will be with Veer, to whom she will explain everything. She will immediately ask him to enquire about James. Will he listen? Yes, he will. After all, they both were, as Veer would say, only victims of circumstances. She was dead sure about one thing- that he truly loved her. She promised herself to behave more maturely now. Oh God! Thoughts were flooding her already tired mind like the rampant waves in an ocean. She closed her eyes.

For yet another time, from a solitary telephone booth, she nervously dialled a phone number and waited. Her hands were still trembling when she heard a male voice at the other end. He wasn't Veer. She was too shocked to speak.

"Hello! Who is there?"

Someone asked. He looked offended for being disturbed so late in the evening.

Somehow, Bhumi regained her senses.

"I am Bhumi. I thought this number belonged to Veer. So..." She said.

"Please hold on."

The voice cut her short.

"Would you please tell me where you are at the moment?" He was asking.

"I...I am..."

She hesitated for a while.

"You need not worry. I am Col. Rajesh. Just tell me where you are."

His voice was reassuring. So Veer has arranged for his best friend. She took a big sigh of relief.

"I just landed at the Delhi airport. I am calling from an STD booth just outside the arrivals."

She looked around and said, "Ok. Listen, you need not go anywhere till I arrive. I will be there before half an hour. Just remain where you are. Is it fine?"

"Yes, I will wait. Thank you so much."

Bhumi managed to say before putting the receiver down. Coming out of the cabin, her mind went back to Veer. Where is he? Why has he given his friend's phone number instead? Maybe he has been posted somewhere outside Delhi. He was talking about it too. Because his best friend was posted here, he gave his number to me. It was the only logical reason she could think about. In any case, she will soon be with Veer, and everything will be alright then. She won't make any silly mistake anymore, she promised herself again.

"Bhumi?"

She was still immersed in deep thoughts when she heard someone call her name. She looked up to find a man who was unmistakably an army officer despite being dressed casually.

"I am Col. Rajesh. Veer is a dear friend of mine," He cordially introduced himself.

She had heard so much about him that he did not feel like a stranger.

"I am sorry to have troubled you at this hour. I thought Veer would be here," She said apologetically.

"I understand Veer did not have the time to tell you anything. Please come with me, I will arrange for your stay."

"I do not understand."

Bhumi was getting apprehensive.

"I will tell you everything. Please come."

Col. Rajesh took Bhumi to one of the hotels that are found in the vicinity of airports. He settled her into a nice room and left but not before promising to return the next morning. He didn't say anything about Veer.

Lying in a lonely hotel room on the outskirts of New Delhi, Bhumi wondered if there was an end to her trials and miseries.

Col. Rajesh came early the next morning. He was dressed formally and carried a briefcase. The first thing he did was to enquire if she had her breakfast and finding that she had none, insisted upon ordering for her. She hardly ate her sandwiches. Col. Rajesh took time to finish his coffee.

In the next half hour, he explained everything to Bhumi, which she found impossible to believe. She felt as if she was in the midst of a dream and Veer would wake her up from it in his gentle ways.

"She was never good with him. In fact, they never had that normal husband-wife relationship. She did not want him as her husband."

She heard Col. Rajesh talking and felt his voice was coming from a distance.

"Then why did she marry?"

Bhumi was puzzled.

"She never wanted to marry Veer; she was forced into it by her parents. And they could find no suitable boy better than Veer after they adopted and raised him as their own son. They never had a son."

"And Veer's family?"

"Oh, he had lost both of his parents in an accident while he was very young. He was adopted by his wife's parents, the late General and his wife."

"Once they found it impossible to control the wild ways of their spoiled daughter, they thought a husband like Veer would change her positively."

"And Veer was ready for that?"

There was a hint of impatience in Bhumi's voice.

"No, he wasn't, as he told me many times. You know Veer better than anyone else Bhumi, you have been the saving grace in his rather sad life, even much before than you came to live with him."

With those words, Col. Rajesh opened his briefcase and presented a file to her. It was the same file that she was looking for on that fateful day in Seychelles when she had lost her unborn child. The file cover was marked as 'Fan' in Veer's handwriting. Bhumi took it so gently as if it possessed a life. Anything that was associated with Veer was dear to her. The file contained all her letters and his replies that Veer had never posted. Tears began to form in her beautiful eyes as she flipped through them.

"The day he landed from Seychelles, Veer gave me this file to be handed over to you."

Col. Rajesh was saying. But Bhumi was not able to hear anything. Her mind was soaked in emotions. Veer had written replies to each one of her letters, and all of them were kept meticulously in that file. The last of the lot was written just before she had come to meet him at Chakrata. She went through the letter, Col. Rajesh waited patiently.

Veer had really opened himself up in that letter. He had written about his strained relationship with his wife, he has also written about his little daughter and how she was the most essential part of his life. In fact, he had written about everything, including his dilemma of agreeing to meet her. Tears in her eyes swelled as she continued to read.

"He never intended to hide anything…"

She was unable to complete her words.

"I have known about you since you began writing fan mails to Veer, Bhumi."

Col. Rajesh was saying. Chocked with emotions, Bhumi couldn't hear him correctly.

"Sometime I would ask him why he never replied, I wasn't aware that he always wrote them. It was only that he never posted his replies."

Bhumi picked up her gaze and looked towards him,

"But why would he do that?"

She was puzzled.

"I don't know. Whenever I asked him, he would say that he couldn't afford to get too involved with his fans and things like that. But with you, it was always different. And he knew that even before he met you for the first time. Maybe you were too young, and he was a matured married man. But a miserable married man and a loner."

"Where is Veer? I have to go to him now."

She regained some composure, her tone was determined.

"I am afraid that is not possible at the moment Bhumi."

"But why?"

She was surprised.

"Because Veer has disappeared and even I do not know where he is at the moment."

"Disappeared?"

Bhumi was more than surprised.

Col. Rajesh nodded in reply.

"But why would he…"

"As there have been 'court-martial' proceedings initiated against him, at the complaint of his …Wife….He wants to clear his name. It was not a criminal conspiracy or a breach of national security, as has been claimed by her. Veer never compromised the security of his country, we both know that."

"So maybe he needs time. Although personally, I do not support this line of action, it can go against him."

Col. Rajesh looked concerned as he said that.

"At least he should have told me…." She pleaded.

"He wasn't sure when would you return; though he knew you would be back. That's why he asked me to receive you."

"I do not know what to do. I have nowhere to go; I can't even go back to my father."

Bhumi seemed to be on the verge of crying.

"I know that Bhumi, but we will have to wait for Veer to come back. I do believe he will appear at the right time. We can only wait until that happens."

"I don't know why God has…"

She couldn't complete her sentence. She was

overwhelmed with emotions.

"You need not worry, I will arrange for everything. Right now, you must get yourself some clothes and other essentials as I see that you carry no luggage. That's understandable given the circumstances. Just give me a few days to sort everything out."

Col. Rajesh got up to leave.

"You know my phone number. Here is another one, it belongs to my office."

He scribbled it on a tissue paper and gave it to Bhumi.

"But call me only when it is absolutely urgent. And you should not utter the name of Veer at the moment, neither on the phone nor in public. I hope you understand. And here is some money, you might need it."

He tried to pass over some money to her.

"No, I do not need it at the moment. I have got the money; I just need to change some dollars."

She remembered the bundle of dollars that was handed over to her by James as she had made the escape. She looked utterly sad.

"That you can do in the hotel lobby itself. Please do not worry, everything will be alright. I am afraid I will be back by tomorrow evening only, around 7 p.m. Let's hope that we have something positive by then."

Col. Rajesh rose from his chair to leave.

"I will be waiting."

Bhumi had regained some of her composure.

Bhumi sat there, motionless for a very long time. Her mind was blank, and she was not able to concentrate on anything. Loneliness had been an integral part of most of her life, except for a brief period when Veer was there. Even that happiness had proved to be extremely short-lived. Now here she was again, feeling like a foreigner in her own country.

She couldn't think of any reason for Veer's disappearance, he wasn't a man who would shy away from facing reality. Or was he? For a moment she doubted if she knew anything about him. She had no idea when he was going to reappear. She longed to be in his comforting arms in that cold hotel room.

She had nothing to do for the next thirty-six hours. She sincerely hoped that Col. Rajesh would have better news when he would be back the following evening. She came back to the present moment and realised that there was a practical problem at hand, she didn't have any clothes to change into. Although she did not feel like going out, she decided to go the market.

She spent her day at the Sarojini Nagar Market in the New Delhi area. It was suggested by the auto-rickshaw driver. The market is known for affordable shopping and is especially popular among the youth. She bought herself some traditional suits, a pair of night pajamas, a pair of chappals and most importantly, some undergarments. The shopping proved to be a distraction from her constant agony, and for a while, she was surprised that she felt good. But soon the feeling turned to guilt as the environment of the city brought back the memory of happily roaming around with Veer not so long ago.

Precisely at 7 in the evening the next day, there was a knock on the door. Bhumi put her diary aside and opened the door to find Col. Rajesh standing outside. His face seemed expressionless, and she couldn't judge if he carried good or bad news with him. As he stepped inside and took a chair, he found her looking questioningly at him. He looked away to find some shopping bags beside the table.

"It is good that you have got something for yourself," He said.

"Where is Veer?"

She was unable to contain her anxiety.

"There is no news of him as yet, Bhumi. Neither has he tried to make contact. I am afraid it will be some time before he makes a comeback. Till then, we will have to make some arrangements."

Col. Rajesh was speaking, but Bhumi's mind had gone into oblivion.

"Are you listening, Bhumi?"

He was trying to bring her back to the present.

"What arrangement?"

She murmured.

"See, you cannot wait for him in a hotel room. There is no guarantee when he will be back. Till then…"

His words were left hanging in the heavy air of the room. She had begun to sob.

"It's getting unbearable for me to live like this."

"I can understand your agony, but I also understand the need of the hour. It is just a matter of time before everything will be fine again."

Col. Rajesh tried to comfort her.

"I do not know what to say or do. I have nowhere to go. I have let everyone down."

"You shouldn't think like that, it's not your fault entirely. Now I have made some arrangements for you."

He took a long pause before continuing further.

"There is a lovely hill station named Ranikhet in the Kumaon hills of Uttar Pradesh. It is also the Kumaon Regimental Centre. A friend of mine is the commanding officer there. He has worked under Veer as well and like me, owes him a lot. His name is Lt. Col. Aakash Bhasin."

The Col. was speaking in a calm voice. Then he stopped to give her a chance to process all the information. She kept her head down.

"There is a vacancy of a primary teacher at Army Public School, Ranikhet. Veer always used to say that you had the qualities of being a good teacher. Bhasin can arrange for you to get that appointment. I think you will like the place, it is a lovely and small hill station and is not so close to your.... home."

He hesitated for a while before completing the sentence. Bhumi had stopped sobbing. Maybe the reality of the situation was beginning to dawn upon her.

"You may take your time to decide. But I think it will be good for you. And it's only a temporary arrangement until Veer is back. This way, I will be able to keep you posted on the developments as well. Take your time; I will be back in the evening."

He rose to leave.

"When should I join?"

She said suddenly, Bhumi had made up her mind, there was no choice. There was a new resolve in those eyes.

"That's good."

"I will be greatly indebted to you for everything."

She was looking directly at him. Col. Rajesh realised why his friend fell for her, it was impossible to deny those eyes.

"No, you must not say that. On the contrary, this is the least I could do, given the circumstances. I will immediately inform Bhasin, he will make arrangements so that everything is in place by the time you reach there. He is a good officer. He knows the situation, you can rely on him. You can go as soon as you wish."

Col. Rajesh completed his words.

"Can I begin coming Monday?"

There were still five good days to go before Monday, it was only Tuesday.

'What a girl who had nowhere to go, would be doing for next so many days?' Col. Rajesh wondered.

"Perfect. Tell me what you need. In that case, you must reach there by Sunday afternoon. I will make immediate arrangements."

The Col. rose to leave.

CHAPTER 12

THE QUEST AND THE WAIT

Col. Rajesh had offered to arrange for her travels that she declined politely. She would reach Ranikhet by Sunday afternoon, she promised.

That evening, she took an overnight bus from ISBT, Delhi to Dehradun and from there, a taxi to Mussoorie. Her heart was thumping as she checked into an obscure hotel on the Camel Back road. The month was February, there was already a hint of spring in the air, but the mountain wind still carried a considerable amount of chill. The old and not so old memories came rushing into her conscious mind. It was hard to believe how much had changed in the last twelve months.

She ventured out of her hotel room in the afternoon, her face half-covered with her dupatta. It was not possible for anyone to recognise her that way, she thought. But she suspected if anyone would care to do so in the first place. She garnered all her courage and thinking about father and Sunita, began to move in the direction where her old world was. It was sickening to know that no one waited for her.

She felt nostalgic when she saw it. There was the old Deodar tree, her former companion. It stood majestically by the roadside as if nothing had changed for him. Bhumi left the road to come closer, and as she gently touched the old companion of her numerous afternoons, she began to cry. The old tree comforted her in his silent ways. He had seen her grow from a small child into a beautiful girl. He was the keeper of most of her secrets. The earth below was covered with lots of its dry leaves. Dropping the leaves was perhaps its way of shedding tears, and if it was so, the old tree seems to have cried a lot in her absence. Bhumi was saddened further.

Many people passed by the road while she once again sat on the lap of the old Deodar tree. There were locals engrossed in their own selves who walked past hurriedly. She could only recognise some of them. There were tourists, busy trying to enjoy the beauty of nature and pleasant weather. No one bothered to look twice towards a young girl sitting alone under a roadside tree. Bhumi felt an immense amount of peace. Time stood still, and she felt that Sunita would soon call her to bombard her with her numerous tales and both the friends would walk back, hand in hand just like the old times.

As it began to get darker after the Sun went behind the mountains, she realised that the times have changed; there was no Sunita out there. Even there was no stepmother waiting to scold her at home. There was no home for her to go to. She got up and embraced the old tree one last time. Unable to garner enough courage to penetrate further into her old world, she decided to go back to her hotel. She felt exhausted.

Bhumi left her hotel room very early the next morning. It was only six in the morning, and the whole town was still sleeping. The mountain towns generally begin their day a bit late than their counterparts in the northern plains owing to their cold weather.

There was merely a hint of light on the horizon just beyond the mountain chains. The mountains themselves looked intimidating at that hour as Bhumi walked hurriedly. She wanted to be there and back before anyone could see her. Last evening, she had felt as if everyone looked at her suspiciously. As if they had recognised her and despised her. She wore the woolen cap, her last day's only purchase that covered most of her beautiful face. She realised that she was almost running as she moved quickly towards her home.

Father might be awake; he always used to get up before his mother. Will he still be going out to fetch fresh morning milk from the nearby shop? Will he recognise her? Will she be able to contain her emotions? Thousands of questions engulfed her already tired mind. She had hidden her face, but how could she put a veil to her persona? If there was one person who would recognise her at any point in life, under any circumstances, it was her father.

Bhumi decided she wouldn't go close enough. If her father comes out of the house at the instant when she is passing by, she will run. And if she sees him coming from a distance, she would turn and walk away. It was impossible for her to walk the other path anymore. Her heart was beating so loud that she was afraid it might stop. Just below the cap, she could feel the perspiration building on her forehead on that chilly morning of fading winters.

It was definitely not her house. She went past it thrice. There was no sign of father cleaning up the veranda or going out for milk. Instead, there was an old man doing some Yoga outside. There was also a bike upfront; father didn't know how to ride a bike. When she was passing through it the fourth time, she also saw an old woman standing outside, perhaps drinking some tea. They looked an old couple and were completely unfamiliar. Now she could clearly see their faces, the daybreak has happened.

Suddenly she realised that something else was missing too. The house looked naked; it was devoid of all of her beloved flower pots. She had planted so many flowery plants and creepers all over the place in all kinds of pots- in empty soft drink bottles and old tin cans. Now they weren't there, they were all gone. It looked so hollow, the place. She felt as if she had lost something precious. Maybe, she didn't deserve them; she had left them behind at their own fate. What else she could expect, she said to herself. She didn't care for anyone, and now the world too has moved on.

She looked across the road and found Sunita's house standing exactly as she had left it. Only it bore a recent whitewash. He remembered that Sunita's family were late risers. She had to fight a sudden urge to go and meet her immediately. But it was getting busier, people had woken up. Some neighbours passed by, looking suspiciously at a girl standing alone on the road with no apparent purpose. Stealing one last glance at what was her only world not so long ago, with heavy feet, slowly she began to move away.

Sunita's mother carried a bagful of vegetables and was moving leisurely towards her house. Bhumi caught her by surprise.

"Bhumi? You?"

She exclaimed as she recognised her.

Bhumi tried to touch her feet, but the lady moved back.

"Aunty Namaste!" She said seriously, hiding her disappointment.

"Where have you been? It's been…"

Bhumi could sense the resentment in her voice. She was trying to avoid her.

"Where has my papa gone aunty?"

She asked hastily as the old lady had begun to walk again.

"Beta I am getting late for lunch."

Sunita's mother tried to ignore her.

"Aunty, please!"

Bhumi moved forward and stopped her in her stride.

"Please talk to me just for a moment, I will go away then," She pleaded.

The old lady thought for a while.

"Ok. But you better hurry up. I have so much work to do."

"Where my papa has gone?" She repeated.

"Your father sold the house within a month of your running away. How could he face the society? And he got himself transferred to some far off place." Sunita's mother said curtly.

"Where?"

"That I don't know. I have heard somewhere close to Uttarkashi."

The lady gestured towards the north, towards the Himalayas.

"And Sunita… Aunty?"

Bhumi hesitated.

"You not only broke your promise, but you also broke her heart. Throughout her marriage ceremony, she kept on looking for you. My poor girl really believed that you would come." She said sarcastically.

Bhumi couldn't say anything immediately. The old lady had begun to move again.

"Where is Sunita now aunty?"

Bhumi asked hurriedly.

"Please spare my daughter now; she is happy in her married life. I beg you should not try to meet her again."

She turned to warn her firmly and then started to walk away from her. She left Bhumi standing with tearful eyes. It wasn't the apathy shown by the old woman that made her emotional; it was the memories of her father and Sunita.

The information that she needed was provided by a common friend. Sunita was married to a government servant who worked at the revenue department and was posted at Vikasnagar in Dehradun. That was where Sunita lived.

There wasn't any business left for her in Mussoorie. Beside the two people who didn't live there anymore, the town did not possess any other charm to hold her. In the evening, she left Mussoorie for Dehradun and once there, checked into a hotel on the Rajpur Road. The very next day, she took a bus to Vikasnagar that was located 30 km towards Chakrata. Vikasnagar is a small satellite town of Dehradun and is a gateway to Chakrata hills. The mention of Chakrata during the bus ride brought her some fond memories. She could never forget that town; it was where everything had started on a stormy night. 'Life seems to have come to a full circle ', Bhumi thought.

Only a year ago, she and Sunita were inseparable. And today, here she was, full of doubts and apprehensions just to meet her best friend. It would not be easy for Sunita to forgive her. Even if she does, a lot depended on her husband, her new family. Life changes a lot for the girls after marriage, she thought. There isn't a free will after that.

Engrossed in her dilemmas, she stepped out of the bus at Herbertpur chowk. According to the girl who had given her the address, Sunita's house was close to the main road towards Vikasnagar. Her father in law was a retired army man and has recently built a house in a locality called 'Sainik Colony'. After a brief inquiry, she decided to walk. There were new constructions all around. Houses were being built on what would have been beautiful paddy fields not very long ago. Now apart from some smaller fields here and there, there stood row of houses on either side of narrow lanes. The development was haphazard, and so were the thoughts developing in Bhumi's head as she moved closer to her destination.

Sunita's house was no different from any other in the locality. In the February sun, Bhumi was perspiring as she reached the house and the hot weather wasn't the only reason.

An old lady opened the front door. At least she looked affable, thought Bhumi.

"Yes?" She asked enquiringly.

"*Namaste ji*. I am...Sunita's friend. She lives here *na ji*?"

Bhumi hesitated as she tried to look inside through the open door. There wasn't a sign of Sunita.

"But I didn't see you at the marriage ceremony."

The old lady, who was perhaps Sunita's mother in law, retorted suspiciously. It was understandable; Bhumi was mentally prepared to be denied ...

"I wasn't in the town at that time aunty. That's why I am here to congratulate her personally."

Bhumi immediately realised it was a wrong statement. What if Sunita had told them everything about her? She had every right to be very angry.

Looking at the gift wrapped in golden paper in her hands, the lady asked,

"What is your name, beta?"

She wasn't still convinced.

"I...Am...Bhumi."

She was unsure of the result her name was going to bring.But that changed everything.

"Bhumi? Are you Bhumi?" The lady exclaimed enthusiastically.

"Please come in beta. Sunita is always talking about you."

She held Bhumi by her hand and led her inside.

"Come and sit. I will just call her. Sunita will be so happy; she is working in the backyard at the moment."

Her mother in law said hurriedly.

Bhumi was still reeling under the effect of a sudden change of atmosphere when she heard a commotion from inside the house. She turned and saw Sunita rushing towards her. As soon as she saw Bhoomi, she froze. Bhumi was still standing helplessly when Sunita came and embraced her. Both friends began to cry. It was some time before they regained composure at the behest of Sunita's mother in law.

"Would you keep crying or welcome your friend?"

The old lady demanded.

There was so much to say, so much to share that even usually chirpy and talkative Sunita fell short for words. They were standing on the terrace and talking happily as if nothing had happened in between. Sunita told Bhumi how she missed her at her marriage. She even told her about her father and the mental tortures he received at the hands of his wife once Bhumi had left. There was also an occasion when her father angrily retorted that his daughter did the right thing by running away from such an environment, told Sunita.

Bhumi felt a great relief. 'So papa understood me after all,' she murmured.

"Why shouldn't he, that lady is such a fake. But now that you are back, everything is going to be perfect again. We are going to have fun again, you see."

Sunita was full of optimism and Bhumi kind of felt good after a long time.

Tea was served by Sunita's mother in law who took the rare initiative by Indian standards to do so, and that surprised Bhumi. There was a certain level of comfort in the house that made her feel happy.

On her part, Bhumi told everything to her best friend.

"Wow! My princes have gone international?"

Sunita exclaimed.

"So you did sit in an airplane? How was that?"

She was really excited and questioned her rapidly. In her old ways, she wanted to know everything at once. She was her Sunita; she hadn't changed a bit. Sunita was particularly interested to know about Dr. James and teased her a lot about him.

"Is he really smart and handsome like a foreigner we see in the movies? How I always wanted to have a foreigner as a boyfriend."

Sunita asked and informed her at the same time. Bhumi tried to discourage her, but she had never been successful at that in the past too.

"Do not worry, the *fauji* uncle must be stuck somewhere. I know these army men well enough now. Even my father in law, who was a *fauji* once, would go to merely buy some vegetables and wouldn't return till evening. *Hai na Ma?"*

Sunita turned and asked her mother in law. The lady could only smile in return.

"You see, he will return alright soon. These important people have important work all the time that we common people can't understand dear."

Her words worked like a balm on Bhumi's battered soul. It was for the first time in several months when she felt good, the unfortunate happenings of the past seemed like a bad dream. Perhaps Sunita was right; the good times were just around the corner.

Hours passed by happily. It was almost evening, and Bhumi decided it was time to leave.

"Leave? Are you mad or what?" Sunita exclaimed.

"I have to go to Suni."

She tried to reason with her best friend.

"And what shall I tell your Jijaji then? That his only sister in law, about whom he has heard so much in past several months, refused to meet him? You are not going anywhere, madam," Sunita declared.

She wasn't ready to listen to her explanations.

"No beta, she won't allow you to go. Nobody can deny her in this house. And she has been waiting for this day for so long. You must stay."

Even her mother in law insisted.

It was impossible to deny such love and affection.

Bhumi felt really great for her. Sunita looked all comfortable in her new home.

"At least one of us is happy." Bhumi thought and stayed for the night.

Ranikhet is another beautiful Cantonment town up in the Kumaon hills of North India. It is about ninety kilometres from Kathgodam, the gateway of Kumaon and the last station of North-eastern Zone of Indian Railways. It is from where the Himalayan ascent begins.

Ranikhet is home to Kumaon and Naga Regiments of the Indian Army. Located at an altitude of 6132 feet above sea level, one can see the beautiful snow-clad western range of the majestic Himalayas from there.

Ironically, the literary meaning of Ranikhet in Hindi is 'Queen's Meadows', and according to the local legend, it got its name because it was here that Raja Sudhardev won the heart of his queen Rani Padmini, who subsequently chose the area as her residence, giving it its present name-Ranikhet.

In 1869, the British established the headquarters of the Kumaon Regiment here and began to use the station as a retreat from the punishing heat of North Indian summers. Even such a beautiful place with its cool and pleasant climate and history laden with love failed to bring peace to Bhumi's mind. She had reached there the day before, having taken the overnight Doon-Kathgodam Express from Dehradun and then a taxi from Kathgodam to Ranikhet.

Lt. Col. Aakash Bhasin was an affable man. He seemed to be in his mid-thirties and lived in a big bungalow on the army campus with his wife and two kids- a son and a younger daughter. Bhumi loved the kids instantly and looked forward to meeting them often as long as she was there. The officer had arranged for her a decent quarter not far from his own residence. It was just outside the gates of the army campus.

The Army Public School, popularly known as APS

Ranikhet was established in the year 1982. It is located in sylvan surroundings, half-hidden from the public eye in the Army Cantonment Board area. It is housed in a typical army styled double-storey building. There are Oak, Pine and Deodar trees all around the campus, some of them standing in the middle of pebbled playgrounds. To Bhumi, they looked like the guardians to the playing children and reminded her of the solitary Deodar tree back, what once was her home.

Bhumi kind of settled down in her new role as the primary school teacher at APS, Ranikhet. In comparison to handling the kids with special needs at the children ward of Seychelles General hospitals, it was a cakewalk. Bhumi loved to spend as much time as possible at school. It was her love, her meditation and her escape.

In the evenings, when she wouldn't be writing her diary or reading Veer's poetry, she would watch the television. It was provided by Lt. Col. Bhasin. Since the opening up of the Indian economy in 1991, the information and broadcasting ministry of Govt. of India had allowed many Private Indian and foreign broadcasters to operate their channels in India. Now, one had a choice to watch any number of them, and some soap operas had become immensely popular among the people. But for Bhumi, she would stick to watching different news channels, looking for some hints or some news about Veer. There wasn't any mention of him but what she did get to know little about was Seychelles. The coup had happened some time back, but there was still a stalemate, and even the Govt. of India was trying to find a favourable solution. The president was ousted alright, but there wasn't news on his only son who was a doctor. Bhumi had already written a series of letters to James, she had even tried calling at his workplace, but all her efforts had proved to be futile. She was yet to receive a reply, and like Veer, she wasn't sure of James's fate too.

Feeling helpless and desperate for some news, Bhumi would go and meet Lt. Col. Bhasin every alternate day. She continuously had to fight an urge to enquire daily, but it would be too much, she had thought. And with the same answers day after day, even the army man felt sorry for her. He sometimes would invite her for dinners at home. His wife was gentle, and kids were adorable, Bhumi loved to tell them stories. The kids liked her too. Lt. Col. Bhasin, having received the inputs from school authorities, was full of praise for Bhumi. She was doing wonderfully well as a teacher.

In spite of all the accolades, Bhumi was tormented from within. Lt. Col. Bhasin often tried to pacify her by telling her that she would be the first person to know about any news on Veer, whenever that happens. But that couldn't stop her from visiting him day after day.

CHAPTER 13

The Penance

Bhumi rushed to the reception to receive the call. She was instantly filled with hope as soon as she was told that there was a phone call from New Delhi for her. Was it possible that Veer was on the line? Yes, it was! He was one such man.

For yet another time in her brief life, Bhumi picked up the phone with trembling hands and found that Col. Rajesh was on the other side.

"Hello!"

Even her voice was shaking as she spoke.

"Hello Bhumi, this is Col. Rajesh."

He spoke in a voice that failed to give any hint of the news that was in his possession.

"Tell me Veer is back *na?*"

She spoke impatiently, it was almost childish.

"There is something that I wanted to share with you Bhumi."

As Col. Rajesh spoke those words, all hopes that she held high in her heart fell down abruptly. His words meant that the news wasn't going to be the one that she hoped to hear.

"What is ...That?"

Bhumi looked terrified.

"Actually last evening, the cops have found Veer's wife Roma dead at one of the hotels here in Delhi."

The Col. Informed.

"What? She is dead?"

Bhumi was taken aback.

"But how's that possible? Wasn't she the one who complained..."

She was surprised that she didn't feel much. Maybe it was because she hadn't met that lady in her life. She had seen her only in some pictures, and that constituted all of Bhumi's knowledge about Veer's wife.

"Yes, she was. The police declared it was due to some drug overdose, she had gone to some party earlier in the evening. But according to my sources, it's a case of suicide."

"Oh! No."

Bhumi now couldn't believe what she was hearing.

"But there's more to it Bhumi,"

She heard Col. Rajesh speaking at the other end.

"Means?"

"She had withdrawn all her complaints against Veer before she died. She even admitted that she had allowed Veer to go with someone...Because they were on the verge of getting divorced anyway."

"I...I can't believe all this."

Bhumi was spellbound. The Colonel spoke further,

"And even this is not all. There is something more that I want you to know."

Bhumi began to shiver with the nervous energy. Words failed to come out of her throat; she could hardly hear the Colonel's voice coming through the phone.

"I have also come to know that the army has dropped the court-martial proceedings against Veer, especially in the light of letter of recommendations sent by the government of Seychelles. They have recognised his timely services in thwarting the military coup against their democratically elected government."

Tears began to roll down Bhumi's eyes. But this time, they were the tears of joy. Col. Rajesh allowed her precious moments of happiness.

Suddenly she asked,

"What about their daughter now? Who is there to look after her now since Veer…"

She was not able to complete her words.

"Not many people, I am afraid. There are some distant relatives but not someone from the immediate family. In any case, the kid was always closer to Veer, and as far as I know, he has secured her future financially."

Col. Rajesh informed.

"But money is not everything. A kid needs love and care, and so much more...

Bhumi spoke from her heart, her voice was dreary.

"You are right Bhumi. That's another problem that we

have to deal with now. But I am sure it is just a matter of time now before Veer is back."

For the first time in several months, Bhumi began to feel that her life was going take a turn and this time, for better. There was silence.

"I will keep you updated."

She sensed that the conversation was coming to an end.

"And where is… Veer's daughter now?"

She asked abruptly.

"Oh! Little Sanaya is studying at a boarding school, she must be in class 5th now."

He spoke fondly of Veer's daughter; it seemed he liked the kid a lot.

"If not for anyone else, Veer should come back for the poor kid. She needs him the most."

"I sincerely believe so Bhumi."

"One last request," Bhumi spoke hurriedly.

"You can be sure if it's possible, I will do it."

Bhumi knew he was speaking the truth.

"If you can get any information about Dr. James Shriram from Seychelles..."

"I will try and let you know."

Col. Rajesh assured her and disconnected the line. The face of James standing helplessly on the lawns of the Presidential palace resurfaced in Bhumi's memories. Now only if she could also find James safe, she would not ask anything from God again, she promised.

Nainital is known for its beautiful lake up in the mountains. The famous Naina Devi Temple stands at the far end of the lake, just beside the pebbled ground that also acts as a stadium for the lovers of cricket and football. That flat part of the town is aptly called 'The Flats' and is the favourite spot for the tourists and vacationers.

Nainital is also famous for its various educational institutions, and the All Saints College is one of the better known among them. It is an all-girls' residential school, and its mission statement says that it strives to provide quality and moral driven education to the girl child and to thus empower the women of tomorrow.

The All Saints College was established way back in 1869 in Nainital at a place known as 'Stoneleigh' where Ramsey hospital now stands. The school eventually got its final home in the Ayarpata Hills in 1892 and exactly after a century, still stood majestically when Bhumi made her entry through its old fashioned gates.

The day was Sunday. It was a day when parents and guardians could visit and meet their wards at the school. It is not easy for an unknown visitor to go and meet a resident student at the All Saints College unless he or she is authorised in writing by either of the parents of the student. Bhumi knew it and was prepared to make a determined effort on her part.

She had taken the first bus that went out of Ranikhet to Nainital that day.

The All Saints College, Nainital is governed by the Holy Family Sisters that falls under the chairmanship of

Bishop of Agra Diocese. The Sister Principal is the head of the institute. Bhumi finds her to be a kind lady who took cognizance of the unusual and unfortunate situation that had happened in the case of that particular student. She was also aware of the fact that there hadn't been any visitors to the student of late and that the child was feeling increasingly lonesome.

Bhumi wasn't authorised to meet the child, but her background as a teacher at one of the well-known schools of the region made it easier for the sister to allow her a brief meeting with the child. It came with a rider; she wasn't allowed to take the student out of the college premises. But that was all that Bhumi had bargained for.

Bhumi had another problem to deal with; she had great personal apprehensions about meeting Veer's daughter. She couldn't think of a way to present herself to the little child. What would she say who she was? She remembered the day when she had come to know about her existence in Veer's life and the unfortunate happenings that had followed afterward. She hated herself for being so self-centered, so indifferent towards the small kid. Now she was determined to make amends, she could relate to the unfortunate child in a way, she knew how it was to lose one's mother so early in life.

Sitting in cold and dull corridors of the administrative wing of that grand building, Bhumi was all occupied in her thoughts when she saw her coming. She was accompanied by the lady warden.

She was unmistakably Veer's daughter. She possessed the same deep-set eyes and sharp features; the resemblance to her handsome father was too profound to be missed. Bhumi was spellbound for more than a moment. The lady went away, leaving the child with her.

The kid was looking directly at her face. She seemed extremely innocent and beautiful; Bhumi resisted a great urge to give her a hug.

"Hello, Sanaya! How are you?" She said lovingly.

"I am fine, thank you."

Even her voice was so sweet and pure. She stood at a distance from her; her eyes were transfixed at her face. Bhumi felt she should have been like her when she was young.

"Do you know who am I?"

She was finding it difficult to make a conversation. She was surprised when little Sanaya nodded in agreement. Bhumi thought she might have mistaken her for some distant relative.

"Then tell me my name."

She was smiling.

"You are Bhumi aunty."

Bhumi was startled, she couldn't think about it even in her wildest dreams. This was impossible, how could she know her name. How could that small child even know that she ever existed? Someone passed by and Bhumi regained her senses after a very long pause.

"How do you know… my name, Sanaya?"

She managed to say in the end.

"Papa told me about you. He showed me your photos when he was here last. And…

"And?"

"He told me that you will come and meet me."

The short hairs at the nape of her neck rising instantly, Bhumi fought hard to control her tears. Veer had so much confidence in her; he shared her identity, her existence with his beloved daughter while she had refused to accompany him back…

"Would you like to come out Sanaya? I am feeling cold."

She feigned a shiver. It brought a little smile on the small face of the kid. She began to walk silently.

Once outside and into the sunshine, Bhumi felt better.

"Let's sit here for a while."

She gestured towards a flight of stairs on the sidelines of the pebbled playground. They both sat side by side.

"Do you love chocolates Sanaya?"

Bhumi smiled.

"Ya, I love chocolates but only the Cadbury ones. Papa will bring me those only."

The kid replied as a matter of fact; her voice was laden with innocence.

"So this is what I have got for you today."

Bhumi took out a pack of Cadbury chocolates from her bag. Sanaya's bright eyes flickered briefly at the sight of her favourite chocolates before they turned sombre again. She was hesitant.

"It's alright Sanaya, they are for you only."

Sensing her dilemma, Bhumi tried to prompt her lovingly. The kid slowly took the pack and kept it to her side. Bhumi didn't insist further.

There was a long pause after that; she found it challenging

to build a conversation again. The kid sat silently.

"Do you like it here?"

"No," Flatly she said.

"The school is not good?"

She tried to make eye contact.

"I want to live with Papa and Mumma and…"

She stopped to speak any further.

"You can tell me, I won't tell anybody, God promise."

Bhumi gestured with her hands, touching her ears and throat. She had seen that in her class, small kids always used to do it with each other those days. It did the trick, the kid spoke again, "No one comes to meet me now. All other kids have their parents coming; they take them out on our night outs. Since mumma left…Even papa has not come…"

The kid was looking extremely sad and lonesome.

"You don't worry Sanaya, papa will be back soon. He might have some important work to do. In the meantime, if you like, I will come and meet you every Sunday."

"Every Sunday? Really?"

The kid smiled, her eyes twinkling again. She was so much like her, getting angry and happy in no time, Bhumi felt.

"Yes, and I will bring you your favourite chocolates too."

"Then all my friends will be jealous of me."

She was smiling brightly.

"They might be, but you can win them by sharing your

chocolates then."

Bhumi said.

"That *toh* I will do. Papa says we must always share."

The kid adored her father; there was no doubt about that. Bhumi felt so good to see her happy again, she felt as if a hefty load was lifted off her soul. She could breathe easily again.

On her way back, she wore a smile all the time. She thought about her innocence, about her resemblance to Veer. She somehow felt closer to him. There was spring in her stride, she had found a purpose to her life, and her whole existence felt lighter after a long long time.

For the next two months, every Sunday, Bhumi would take the first bus from Ranikhet to Nainital to be the first among the parents visiting their wards at the All Saints College, Nainital. Her days were spent planning her weekend trips, buying little things that would make little Sanaya happy. Each meeting brought both of them closer and closer. Sanaya had begun to like her as well, Bhumi felt. 'You are just like an angel', she told her once. She remembered that James once spoke about her like that. She reminded herself to think about Veer. There was still no trace of him, but his absence didn't haunt Bhumi like it used to. He needed her to look after his little Sanaya in his absence, she would think. In a way, both of them were drawn towards each other and Veer was the force that bound them together, even in his absence.

The television failed to bring any news of him. They were unable to deliver any news of James as well. The stalemate at the small island nation of Seychelles had culminated, and fresh elections were scheduled to take place in the future, which was all they would say. There was no news on the former President or his family. New important headlines occupied the news space, and a small island nation was not big news when a lot was happening around the world. But Bhumi still watched it as diligently as she wrote letters to James. Ever since she met Sanaya, Bhumi somehow had a constant feeling that the time was not far when she will get the news that had eluded her all those months. She would write everything in the diary that was her constant companion.

She would still go and meet Lt. Col. Bhasin every now and then who was always full of praise for her. Bhumi was presented with the best teacher award at the raising day ceremony of the school, and her kids had won the best presentation prize. She was liked by the parents and was doing wonderfully well professionally. She regularly wrote letters to Sunita as well, explaining all the happenings of the week. Everything was going to be great again, as she predicted, Sunita had written back. It was just a matter of time when Veer will come back and clear his name. Then they all will go and meet her father, there was no way he could deny his beloved daughter, Sunita had said in one of her letters.

There was no reason not to believe her best friend, Bhumi thought and smiled.

September was coming to an end. The rains had subsided, leaving behind a sheet of greenery all over the mountains that looked heavily laden with all kinds of green vegetation. Some of them had begun to shed their leaves, and many of the mountain trails were now covered with dry leaves of beautiful brown and orange shades. One could still see all shades of green in a single glance. October was going to be the month of festivals; people had started preparing for the 'Ram Leela'. Dussehra was to be celebrated in a fortnight, and young boys and girls could be seen going door to door collecting donations from all God-fearing citizens of the town.

Bhumi had written to Col. Rajesh to somehow arrange for a night out for Sanaya. The poor girl needed it as all other boarder students were going out with their parents every month. Secretly in her heart, Bhumi wanted to show her own world to the kid. She had made all the plans for that day, only Col. Rajesh was yet to get back with the permission. She was confident that he was capable of doing that.

Bhumi was writing her diary when she got the call. It was for the first time since she had come to Ranikhet when Lt. Col. Bhasin called for her. Finally, Col. Rajesh had got the permission, she thought as she walked hurriedly towards the offices of the Commanding Officer. Lt. Col. Bhasin will meet her at his office, she was told by the *sahayak*.

CHAPTER 14

The Renunciation

Lt. Col. Bhasin was behind his desk. As soon as he saw Bhumi at the door, he gestured her to come inside and have a seat. Bhumi, still wearing the saree that she had worn to the school, looked questioningly at the army man who strangely, looked distracted.

"Is everything alright?"

She had begun to feel that something was not normal. It was confirmed when he started to speak.

"Bhumi, what I am going to tell you is still an unconfirmed report. But as I have promised that you will be the first person..."

Bhumi's heart sank; she couldn't hear him any further.

"Bhumi, Bhumi... are you listening?"

He tried to bring her back to the present. Her eyes wore the fear of the unknown.

"It is not a piece of bad news that you fear, in fact, it is good news."

She heard him say and immediately became attentive.

'Tell me, Veer is alright."

She couldn't help herself disclose her worst fears.

"That Col. Veer should be. I have called you to tell something that no one else knows till now. I might be breaking a few rules, but this is the least I can do for him. Now listen to something that you will have to keep to yourself only."

Lt. Col. Bhasin lowered his voice. He looked serious, and Bhumi nodded like a small kid.

High up in the Himalayas, there lies the holy town of Badrinath in the Chamoli district of Uttarakhand, the abode of Gods. The town is situated in a valley along the Alaknanda River at an elevation of 3300 meters above sea level. The famous temple town, repeatedly destroyed by earthquakes and avalanches since ancient times, was re-established by Adi Sankaracharya in the 7th century and today, Hindus (especially the Vaishnavites) come in large numbers to pay their homage to Lord Badrinarayan.

There are many legends associated with Badrinath. According to Bhagwat Puran, 'There in Badrikashram, the supreme being(Vishnu) is in the incarnation as the sages Nara and Narayana have been doing great penance since time immemorial for the welfare of all living entities.' The mountains around Badrinath are mentioned in Mahabharata where Pandavas were said to have expired one by one when ascending the slopes of a peak called 'Swargarohini' (The ascent to heaven). The Pandavas passed through Badrinath and the village of Mana on their way to Swarga. There is also a cave today in Mana where, according to the legend, Rishi Ved Vyas wrote the Mahabharata.

The area around Badrinath was celebrated in Padam Purana as abounding in spiritual energy and even today, many sages visit and stay in the mountains around the valley in search of truth and enlightenment.

But there is another beauty to Badrinath, people and pilgrims find themselves intimidated by the sight of one of the most beautiful mountain peaks towering dramatically and majestically from just behind the main temple over and above the entire holy town and the valley.

That mountain peak is called 'Neelkantha.' Standing nine kilometres to the east of Badrinath at an elevation of 6507 meters, the majestic mountain peak, according to the legend, wasn't there in ancient times. In its place, there was an adjacent route between Kedarnath and Badrinath and the Purohits and worshippers of the two most sacred temples could worship both the Gods in a single day. But due to some sins caused by a worshipper, lord Shiva became displeased with them and blocked the route by putting a colossal sky kissing mountain there.

Today, the same mountain peak is known as Neelkantha, a jewel or the name given to Shiva with a blue throat, the result of his drinking the poison that emerged from the churning of the ocean or 'Samudra Manthan.' The peak is surrounded by many famous glaciers- the Satopanth glaciers on its north-west side; the Panpatia on its south-west and on its west lays the famous Gangotri glacier.

Though this beautiful peak stands only 6500 odd meters in height today, it is not an easy one to climb, and only a handful of successful ascents have been reported till date. Purportedly it was first climbed only on the 13th of June, 1961 by a team of Indian army led by Col. Narinder Kumar from its north face. Then again on the 3rd June 1974, led by Sonam Pulzor, a mountaineering team of Indo Tibet Border Police reached the summit.

The next ascent of Neelkantha took place only in 1993 by an international team led by Col. H.S. Chauhan and no fewer than 32 climbers, many of them from the Indian army, reached the difficult summit between 31st May and 2nd June. Naib Subedar Devi Singh of the 17th Kumaon was one of them.

That multinational army venture was to attempt the summit from its virgin north-east ridge. The team left

New Delhi on the 5th of May and reached to establish an intermediary camp at a place known as 'Charan Paduka' three kilometres east of Badrinath. The day was the 9th of May, 1993. The next day, as the team moved from the intermediary camp towards establishing its first base camp just beneath the towering Neelkantha, something startled Naib Subedar Devi Singh on his way. It happened so quickly that he did not get enough time to think.

Once they established their base camp in the afternoon, the next few days were meant for acclimatisation. Devi Singh continued to think about the incident, trying to remember everything. It was only in the dead of the following night that he reached the conclusion that he couldn't make a mistake. The next day, Devi Singh ventured out to establish the truth.

The same Naib Subedar Devi Singh now stood in the office of Lt. Col. Aakash Bhasin repeating once again the fascinating findings of his rendezvous that day. Bhumi was sitting spellbound.

'How could you be so sure that the Sadhu you met that day was none other than Col. Veer Pratap Singh?"

Col. Bhasin was asking.

"Sir, I have been Saheb's 'sahayak' for more than four years. I even went with him when he was transferred once. I was responsible for all his personal things. I could not make a mistake. He was Saheb alright and then also..."

Devi Singh looked confident.

"Tell me the full incident, Devi," Lt. Col. Bhasin ordered.

"Sir, as we moved from our camp at Charan Paduka that day, a sadhu hurriedly passed by us on the slopes. He was carrying some wood that he might have collected from the nearby jungle. I instantly felt that I have seen that face and suddenly I remembered that it was Saheb's face.

As we established our first base camp a few kilometres up, I kept on thinking about that sadhu so much so that I could not sleep that night. How could Saheb be there so high up in the Himalayas? Why would he be disguised as a sadhu? All these questions haunted me throughout the night. In the end, I was confident it was none other than Saheb. Saheb had once been very ill when he was posted at Mau and had developed a beard. It was the same face."

Naib Subedar Devi Singh drew the complete attention of both his audiences.

They were spellbound.

"What did you do then, Devi?" Col. Bhasin asked in anticipation.

"Sir, we were free for the next two days, so I decided to descend to the area where I have last seen Saheb. After roaming for a few hours without any success, there I saw him again. He was moving upward hurriedly through the trees. Again it was the same gait. As soon as I saw him, I shouted, "Saheb!"

As he stopped and turned towards me, I gave him a salute. And you know what Sir? …He returned my salute and then hurriedly walked away."

Lt. Col. Aakash Bhasin stood up from his chair. 'Old military habits die hard.' He said to himself.

"Then?"

"I followed him then sir. He moved very fast indeed and ultimately vanished inside what looked like a cave, Sir. It was tough terrain, and that cave isn't visible easily to anyone. I had great difficulty in marking the route. But I did it, sir."

Devi Singh completed his incredible statement.

"Please tell the place and the route and how to reach that place. I need..."

Unable to contain her excitement, as Bhumi began to speak, her voice quivered. Col. Bhasin immediately gestured her to stop talking. She was sitting at the edge of her chair and could feel exhilaration building up inside her.

After getting all the information from the man, Lt. Col. Aakash Bhasin dismissed Naib Subedar Devi Singh but not before ordering him to remain quiet about the incident until the next order.

"Listen Bhumi!"

He turned to speak to her.

"I know you want to find Col. Veer at the earliest. But I am afraid you will have to do it before anyone else does so. As things stand, even I won't be able to hide the news for long. But I can give you a head start of a few days."

Bhumi rose to leave, she did not have any time to waste.

Bhumi left Ranikhet early the next morning and reached Kathgodam by the afternoon. She intended to reach Haridwar, the door to the Gods at the earliest but there was no bus leaving for Haridwar at that hour. She was unable to spend her time in peace, and many people around the small and cramped bus station looked suspiciously and interestingly at a beautiful girl wandering around aimlessly. She took the first night bus to Haridwar that left Haldwani that day and reached her destination very early the next morning.

When you see Haridwar through the Ganges and all the holy temples and ghats on her banks, it's quite different from the one that presents itself at its bus and railway station. They can easily belong to any other Indian town for that matter. The only difference is created by the hoards of pilgrims that throng the Holy city throughout the year. That morning, Bhumi found that no bus goes to Badrinath directly from Haridwar; maybe a few were leaving from Rishikesh. She took a local bus to the nearby holy city of Rishikesh only to find that it was impossible to reach Badrinath by bus in a single day, it was almost three hundred kilometres up in the Himalayas. At best, she could reach Srinagar in the Garhwal hills.

Taking a night halt in Srinagar, Bhumi could only reach Badrinath by the next evening. October had arrived and the pilgrim season was coming to an end. Most of the inhabitants were beginning to move out of the holy town to save themselves from the freezing winters where temperatures could go as low as minus twenty degrees on the Celsius scale. The shrine was going to be closed soon, and the city was beginning to wear a deserted look.

Soon there would only be a handful of sadhus living in the ashrams and in some caves, someone told her. Bhumi had taken shelter at one of the ashrams in the town. She was utterly exhausted by the time she hit the bed that night. She was continuously travelling for the last sixty hours and felt sick from traversing the tortuous winding roads of the mountains. Sleep eluded her through the night. Based on the information provided by Naib Subedar Devi Singh, she had prepared some notes as well as a map of the area where Veer was spotted last. Now so close to the area, doubts began to creep inside her tired mind. It was almost three months since then. What if he had moved from his hideout? Now that she knew that most people were leaving the area, maybe Veer had already left it too. What will she do if she fails to find the cave? Even if she does, and it proves to be an empty one, then? 'I will go and ask each and every person living in the area. Someone must have seen him.' She tried to regain some positivity before fatigue got the better of her consciousness.

Charan Paduka actually is a beautiful rock that is believed to contain the foot impressions of Lord Vishnu. It is perched at an elevation of 3380 meters above sea level. Positioned at Narayan Parvat, one has to trek uphill for three kilometres from Badrinath to reach there. The path to Charan Paduka is full of various caves and boulders. But the cave that Bhumi was looking for that day, according to Devi Singh, lied further beyond. Bhumi was exhausted by the time she reached Narayan Parvat. She was determined to find Veer, and before embarking on the journey in the morning, she had promised herself that she wouldn't return without seeing him.

As she moved further up, the weather changed, and there were clouds all around. There wasn't a soul in sight, and she struggled to find the arrow marks engraved by Devi Singh on the trunks of high altitude trees. Snowfall had happened a fortnight ago, and the ground was slippery. In her desperation, Bhumi had failed to prepare herself to trek on such dangerous grounds. Utterly exhausted, she tried to consult her notes, only to find them inadequate. She was frustrated; it was proving impossible to find her way. She looked around, there was nowhere to go. The freezing temperature began to take a toll on her body, she found it unable to move her feet. With exhaustion and cold, she was unable to think, her whole body felt numb, and she struggled to remain conscious.

Bhumi could feel the death; it was just a matter of time. She began to breathe heavily; she knew she wouldn't be able to survive. Was she destined to die without meeting Veer? Those were her last thoughts as she began to lose her consciousness.

As Bhumi was about to hit the ground, she was held by a pair of strong hands. She opened her eyes one last time and saw Veer, who was holding her in his arms.

CHAPTER 15

Love Will Always Be There

Five months later...

In April the following year, when the villagers returned at the onset of summer, they remembered the revered sage who lived in a cave up in the mountain. He was meditating there since last year when they had found him on their return last winters. He was definitely a sacred soul since he seemed to have miraculously survived through the freezing cold. No one knew when and from where had he arrived. Since then, the villagers used to visit the sage often, giving him food and alms. But he was always reluctant, and that added to the mystery surrounding his being.

One fine day, led by their headman, a bunch of villagers began their uphill trek to visit the revered soul and seek his blessings. They were astonished by the scene outside the cave. Covered with snow, the sage they held so high in their esteem laid dead and that too in the arms of a young girl.

He was a con man, indeed!

No one visited that con man's cave for the next twenty years!

The End!

During the last few months, the city has received unprecedented rainfall. On my part, I have tried to keep pace with the falling rains, showering all the words that I could to tell you the story that I have promised in the beginning. It is the story of Bhumi and Veer and all those whose destinies were woven together, including mine.

The monsoon has subsided, there is no more rain in the air. Even I do not possess the words anymore and therefore, the story has come to its end. It has entirely been based on the diary that I mysteriously found in that abandoned cave in the Himalayas. Before I began to write, I tried my best to confirm its details, to authenticate its contents. And today I can confidently say that most of the incidents mentioned by Bhumi in her personal diary have been more or less true. This story is an effort to correct a small piece of history and that piece now rests in your, my reader's hands at the moment. Of course, I had to change the names and places as I have no right to play with anyone's reputation.

Yours'

Siddhanth.

Siddhanth, the freelance mountaineer and the blogger, stopped typing and pulled his chair away from his workstation. He looked at his watch, it was almost midnight. He leaned back on his chair and rubbed his tired eyes with his fingers. He then closed his eyes and stayed like that for several moments. Finally, he looked around his dimly lit and sparsely furnished room. Apart from the computer table and a couch, there wasn't much furniture in the room. What it did have in plenty were the books of all kinds. They were everywhere.

Sid finally got up from the chair and came to stand at the solitary window. Almost six feet tall with athletic built;

he looked imposing as he stood against the glass panes. He caressed his small beard with his fingers; it was the constant feature of his handsome face. Once again, he could see the flickering lights at a distance. But unlike the last time, those lights did not belong to some mountain hamlet. They were the city lights and were possessed by the people living in cage like urban dwellings. Will these city people be able to relate to the story that belonged to the mountains? Since the turn of the 21st century, a lot had changed everywhere. During the last decade only, love had been replaced by the lust and like everything else; each story was now measured in terms of its marketability.

Sid remembered an old literary saying,

"The greatest stories ever told are the greatest stories ever sold."

But this story was not about money, he felt he was just an instrument at the hands of almighty that had used him to bring divine justice. He remembered the pair of golden deer, there was no other explanation for the existence of those beautiful creatures.

Siddhanth came back to his workstation and began to type an e mail-

"Dear Publisher,

As promised, here I am sending you the final manuscript of my work in romantic fiction. I trust you will find it good enough for publication…"

One year later…

For the last six months in a row, 'Veer Bhumi' constantly found itself in most of the bestsellers lists. It was also on the 'top ten' list of the Amazon kindle downloads. In a country of more than a billion people, Sid or Siddhanth became a household name. He was the new rockstar of the Indian literary world. More than three hundred thousand copies of the book were sold in the first twelve weeks of its publication. This was a sort of record for a rookie writer. He was invited for the book launches, for inaugurations, to deliver lectures in the colleges and university campuses around and country and off course, to the literary festivals and seminars. He was all over Twitter, Instagram and the internet. There were also talks of making a Bollywood movie based on the story.

The awards came thick and fast too and then came the big one. Tata Literature Live! Festival or simply The Mumbai Litfest is an acclaimed literature festival that takes place in Mumbai every year. Along with the four day celebrations of literature, the festival also awards writers in seven different categories including the 'First Book Award' and 'Book of the Year Award,' the latter being more prominent of the two. It was constituted to recognise noteworthy work in the Indian literary space across fiction and non-fiction genre.

Because of its growing popularity, the Tata Literature Live! Festival is now simultaneously held at three different locations across Mumbai- at the glorious National Centre for the Performing Arts or simply the NCPA campus, the iconic Prithvi Theatre at Juhu and lately at the SPICE institute campus in Bandra, the queen of Mumbai suburbs.

The National Centre for the Performing Arts is located

at the Nariman Point in Mumbai, just opposite to the Marine Drive Jogging Tracks. This magnificent building by the seafront has a number of auditoriums, theatres and spaces where a number of functions, performances and exhibitions are held throughout the year. The Tata Literature Live! Festival is held at the Tata Theatre located inside its premises. The splendid theatre has a seating capacity of 1010 seats and that day, it was filled to its capacity. The month was November and the occasion was the announcement and distribution of literary awards.

That year, the 'Book of the Year–Fiction' award went to Siddhanth for his work in English fiction titled "Veer-Bhumi." The entire jury that constituted of prominent writers, academics, critics, journalists and media personalities was unanimous in their decision. When Siddhanth was called on to the stage to receive the award, he was met with the longest applause of that grand evening. He was quite a handsome man and had a huge fan following among the burgeoning women readers of the country. His dedication and his conviction to bring justice to unheralded lovers of the yore was another reason why he was such a hit among masses, especially the youth.

The chief guest for the evening was the longest serving editor of popular English daily and an iconic figure of the literary world. There was another jury member on stage to present the award that was in the form of a certificate in a dark coloured wooden frame. Siddhanth was called on to the stage to receive the award. As he was to be presented with the award, Siddhanth asked for the mike from the compère. The audiences went silent in anticipation. As he spoke, his voice was clear and definite,

"I am so very happy to receive this special award and I am so thankful to the jury members who found the story of Bhumi and Veer good enough to be appreciated in this manner. Of course, it all started with a personal passion for me to bring this story to the world but let me confess that it was not easy out there. Many a time, especially when the story didn't move further, I would lose sight and direction. But there was one person who stood by me all the time. Who believed more than me in my capacity to …find the truth and write it too. Someone I met on the way and who now has become an integral part of my life. That is one person who really deserves this award more than me. Ladies and gentlemen and honourable jury members, with your permission, to receive this award on my behalf, I would like to call upon stage my dear wife- Dr. Sanaya Shriram Singh. And yes, she is the daughter of Late Col. Veer Pratap Singh and the adopted daughter of Dr. James Shriram, the current President of Republic of Seychelles."

There was an uproar that was followed by huge applause. All eyes went among the audiences to search for her. Slowly she rose from among the crowd, a combination of beauty and elegance. She was Veer's Sanaya but she was also Bhumi's Sanaya. But more than anyone else, she was James's Sanaya who had raised her as his own daughter. A pair of thousand eyes followed her as she moved on to the stage but no eyes could match the love that shone in the eyes of Siddhanth.

Later...

The weather was clear and the Sun shone brightly. It was a beautiful day in the mountains. The President was on a personal visit but still, elaborate arrangements were made at Badrinath. It was not entirely uncommon for a Hindu, even if he was a President of some country, to visit one of the most revered Hindu pilgrimage sites. What was uncommon though, was his desire to visit beyond the shrine.

Later in the day, a function was held in the mountains behind Badrinath which was attended, among others, by Retd. General Rajesh Kumar, Siddhanth, Sanaya, Sunita and her husband and the villagers which were led by their old headman.

The occasion was the rechristening of 'Con man's cave' as "Veer Bhumi" at the hands of Dr. James Shriram, the President of Seychelles.

No one saw a pair of golden deer that intently watched everything from a distance.

High above, the magnificent peak of 'Neelkantha' was shining bright as gold!

The Real End!